FURIOUS MOOSE OF THE WILDERNESS

That independent young wilderness trapper, Pete Gant, met the challenge of a monstrous bull moose with courage and skill—after he let it chase him up a tree and keep him there all night! He was not so sure of his tactics when it came to dealing with Hailey Zulski, tiny and teasing, who could nevertheless work staunchly beside her invalid father, a refugee from Poland, on their rugged sheep ranch.

This was especially the case when Hailey said she would never speak to Pete again if he killed the furious moose in a spirit of hatred and revenge, when he knew perfectly well that she helped her father stock their thin larder with game to tide them over the winter. Then there was the question of books. Pete could read all right, but he needed to know what he was reading, the way the Zulskis did.

This outdoor adventure story has a most unusual slant, but, with Jim Kjelgaard as the author, the reader is assured of stirring action and a true feel of the widerness that is echoed in Mort Künstler's fine illustrations.

Books by Jim Kjelgaard

BIG RED
REBEL SIEGE
FOREST PATROL
BUCKSKIN BRIGADE
CHIP, THE DAM BUILDER
FIRE HUNTER
IRISH RED
KALAK OF THE ICE
A NOSE FOR TROUBLE
SNOW DOG
THE STORY OF GERONIMO
STORMY
COCHISE, CHIEF OF WARRIORS
TRAILING TROUBLE
THE EXPLORATIONS OF PERE MARQUETTE
THE SPELL OF THE WHITE STURGEON
WILD TREK
OUTLAW RED
THE LOST WAGON
THE COMING OF THE MORMONS
LION HOUND
CRACKER BARREL TROUBLE SHOOTER
TRADING JEFF AND HIS DOG
DESERT DOG
HAUNT FOX
THE OKLAHOMA LAND RUN
DUCK-FOOTED HOUND
DOUBLE CHALLENGE
SWAMP CAT
THE LAND IS BRIGHT
RESCUE DOG OF THE HIGH PASS
HI JOLLY!
WOLF BROTHER
WILDLIFE CAMERAMAN
ULYSSES AND HIS WOODLAND ZOO
TIGRE
FAWN IN THE FOREST AND OTHER WILD ANIMAL STORIES
TWO DOGS AND A HORSE
FURIOUS MOOSE OF THE WILDERNESS

FURIOUS MOOSE O

ILLUSTRATED BY MORT KÜNSTLER

THE WILDERNESS

By Jim Kjelgaard

DODD, MEAD & COMPANY, *New York*

The characters and situations in this book are wholly fictional and imaginative: they do not portray and are not intended to portray any actual persons or parties

Library of Congress Catalog Card Number: 65-11810

Printed in the United States of America
by The Cornwall Press, Inc., Cornwall, N.Y.

CONTENTS

1

THE FIRST MEETING

THE SKY was cloudless, but its depths wore a deceptive veil that reminded Pete Gant of a lake sheathed in clear, snow-free ice. A fisherman who looked carelessly from a distance might never realize the ice was there and think he could cast a plug or spinner. But an experienced observer would note signs, such as the absence of waterfowl and waves, to tell him of ice. Just so, there were signs in the sky that told of winter and cold to be.

Among them was a flock of geese in V formation, flying so high that their gabbling drifted to earth as muted squawks. Then there were squirrels scurrying frantically to lay up more food; dejected aspens that clung desperately to a few forlorn leaves; the way the wind sang in the spruces.

Most infallible sign of any, Pete decided, was the way he felt. Spring on the Wisbayah watershed was delightful enough, for then a fellow could pull his traps and be about his fishing. That was always important because the dogs lived on salted or smoked fish all winter—in some lean years the trapper fell back on the same diet. Summer was for loafing, repairing cabins, more catching and salting or smoking fish, if a man didn't get enough in the spring, also visiting town or doing odd jobs for pay—in case he felt like it.

But, even though they brought no obligations except necessary chores, Pete always felt somewhat restricted in springtime and summer. He could not explain it satisfactorily, but he'd wake up at midnight, or three o'clock in the morning, with an uncomfortable feeling that he needed air, and rush outside to breathe. It was almost the way he felt when he tarried in Spruce Crossing too long. If Spruce Crossing was not much as towns went, sometimes it was more than eighteen-year-old Pete could stand.

The wind, that had been coming in fitful gusts from the west, veered suddenly to the north and turned colder. Pete raised his head to take it full in the face, and a smile as effortless as breathing parted his lips. He understood the north wind. It told him of deep drifts, and long trails, and prowling lynx, and many things that would have troubled his heart forever if he had not gone out to meet them in their own land and seen for himself how they were.

Pete shifted the rifle in his hand, shrugged his forty-pound pack into a more comfortable position, and hurried his steps. He'd left Spruce Crossing before dawn yesterday and slept last night at Halfway Cabin, thirty miles out. Tonight, if all went well, he'd stay with Casimir and Hailey Zluski, then go on to his base camp at Two Moose Lake tomorrow. Pete spoke to the dog beside him.

"Last night in civilization, Baldy. Better make the most of it because it's the big woods from tomorrow on."

The dog, a huge crossbreed with a dominant strain of husky,

wagged a responsive tail but did not glance up. The dog beside Pete, as well as the two tagging behind, also carried packs. Wearing harnesses with a rucksack on either side and a third strapped across the top, all three animals looked almost ludicrously overburdened, in spite of their size—the runt of the trio weighed eighty-five pounds. Pete looked affectionately at Baldy.

Despite other means of transportation, a trapper's dogs remained indispensable. It would be impractical, to say the least, to land a plane wherever a trap might be set. Not even horses were useful when the snow lay very deep. For some specialized purposes, dogs continued to be not merely the best but the only practical means of transportation in the wilderness.

Baldy was the lead dog, which, in effect, made him Pete's right arm. Not that it was necessary to entertain any illusions. Big, courageous, and intelligent, in any emergency Baldy would look to himself first. That was what his master expected, and it was what Baldy expected. Pete had never speculated, however idly, on dramatic escapes from death with Baldy in the hero's role. The very tendency to watch out for himself was the principal factor that made this dog worth double his weight in prime lynx.

Quite apart from his practical value as a beast of burden, Baldy was priceless on the winter-locked trails. Storms rose so swiftly that minutes alone elapsed from the first down patter of flakes to a howling blizzard and zero visibility. Under

such conditions no man could possibly find a trail, but Baldy never missed. Many times he had saved Pete the inconvenience of a night's camp in a winter storm and possibly he had even saved his master's life. The fact that he did it because he himself preferred a warm kennel and knew where to find one was unimportant. Nor did the very real and mutual dog-master affection that existed between the two have any part of this. Baldy was a trail dog by instinct, a leader because he could whip both his teammates. Pete could not have lived as he did without such a dog.

The other two dogs, Jake and Megap, were important because they were strong animals whose power Pete needed and could harness. As liabilities, they were accomplished cache robbers, ardent rabbit hunters, and gifted with an uncanny

knowledge of exactly how much they could get away with safely. They carried packs because they were not stupid. Both knew that their packs were on until their master chose to take them off and that a pack-burdened dog can get into serious trouble if left to his own devices. But if they were harnessed to the toboggan, neither would pull his own weight if Pete inadvertently forgot his whip to snap over their heads as a reminder of their duty. Jake was gray and wolflike. Megap, of undetermined ancestry, was covered with kinky black fur that gave him a marked, but most inappropriate, resemblance to a lamb. Megap was the only dog Pete had ever owned who would wag amiably up to an unsuspecting stranger, then snarl warningly at the hand that was extended to caress him! He had an instinct to be friendly, yet trusted nobody but his young master, as a result of a puppyhood haunted by cruelty until Pete had bought him.

The sun passed the high-noon mark and began its curve toward the western horizon. It would be no long journey. Even in September, the days were markedly shorter and, from now until late December, the sun would shine for a few minutes less every twenty-four hours. Sometimes, when the winter sky was overcast, there seemed to be no real day but only a lessening of the night. Conversely, when the days grew longer, they took giant strides. In summer it was often possible to sit outside a half-hour before midnight and read a book or magazine without excessive eyestrain.

Twenty minutes after noon Pete stopped beside a bubbling spring and leaned his rifle against a tree. Discarding his own pack, he eyed the dogs and pondered the advisability of relieving them of their burdens. He decided against it. He'd made good time and it was only about seven miles to the Zluski homestead. The dogs knew that as well as he did. Set free, they might decide to proceed on their own initiative and let him worry about getting the packs in. The dogs could lie down and rest.

All three promptly did so, each choosing a place to his liking and dozing off at once. There was nothing special to excite them and this was just a routine lunch stop. Presently, they would resume the march. All three knew this, and all were too experienced not to take fullest advantage of any opportunity to rest.

Pete built a fire and filled his kettle with water. While waiting for it to come to a boil, so he might properly brew tea strong enough to gag anyone but a wilderness trapper, he lost himself in memories of his first journey over this trail.

That was two years ago, just past his sixteenth birthday. with extensive trapping experience in the backwoods and cutover behind him, he had been, at last and happily, on his way to the real wilderness. He had heard, of course, about the Zluski homestead on the Wisbayah River but nothing had prepared him for what he found there.

A giant with a hooked nose, drooping gray mustaches, and a brigand's haughty stare, no one knew where Casimir Zluski came from or why he was here, and no one had seen fit to ask. Rumor made him a refugee from strife-ripped Poland, and asserted that he had killed anywhere from six to sixty men with his bare hands. He'd started a sheep ranch on the Wisbayah, sixty miles from the nearest market and that market Spruce Crossing, because he was crazy or—according to how one preferred his melodrama—because he had a price on his head and this was a good place to hide.

No less astonishing than Casimir was his motherless daughter and only child. Christened Helen, affectionately called Hela by her father and Hailey by everyone else, she was fourteen when Pete first came to the Zluskis, with a dark and winsome loveliness that seemed created exclusively for her. She was lithe and quick as a fawn. She had a great supply of books which she read hungrily, but, even now, Pete did not know that her father was her teacher and he would not have believed it if someone told him. There was no logical way to reconcile the huge Casimir, who could bring a wild young colt in from the range and fight it to a standstill, with formal education.

Pete had gone on to run his traps from a base camp at Two Moose Lake. Returning in the spring with a respectable catch of fur, he was mildly astonished to reach the Zluski place and be greeted by a lively, lovely Hailey. Throughout the winter he had thought of her, but only when he was again facing her did it occur to him that nothing so fragile should have been able to survive winter in such a place.

Nor could he rid himself of a feeling that Hailey should spend her winters somewhere besides here. Spring and summer—and perhaps the early fall—were the only seasons she should be around these rugged parts.

Although Pete still had not asked Casimir where he came from, it was unnecessary to ask why he was here. Casmir Zluski lived where he did for the same reason Pete had turned to the wilderness—he needed plenty of room.

So did Hailey, but, because she was a girl, she was somehow different. In the first place, she was so tiny. The top of her dark head came two inches below Pete's shoulder and, if he chose, he could encircle her slim waist with his two hands. Not that he ever chose! She was by far the prettiest girl Pete had ever seen, and yet, year by year, she had not only accumulated books but she read and understood them. With a tongue as nimble as her feet, she delighted in teasing Pete and sometimes succeeded in bewildering him. Possessing a great store of amazing ideas, which she expressed at the least provocation—and sometimes at none—she might have angered him, if he were capable of becoming seriously interested in any girl, which he was *not!* Even so, he often worried about her. It still seemed to him that nothing as delicate as Hailey could survive a savage winter in a savage land. It was a relief when spring came and he found out, once again, that she had somehow lived to greet the season that seemed more her own.

Pete drank a final cup of scalding tea, repacked his lunch gear, shouldered his pack, and caught up his rifle. The dogs rose slowly and took their proper places, Baldy falling in beside his master and Jake and Megap behind. All three seemed

more eager, not because of the short rest, which they hadn't really needed, but because they were near the Zluskis' and a longer rest. Pete was not the only one who knew this trail. His dogs had also been this way.

Rising to the crest of a wooded ridge, Pete swung down a gentle slope that led to the Wisbayah. It was three and a half miles from here, and, even though there was not a great deal of the day remaining, it was still long before bedtime. There would be man talk with Casimir and, Pete grinned briefly, plenty of opportunity to dodge Hailey's verbal darts. Not that he ever succeeded in emerging unwounded, but there'd never been serious wounds.

Suddenly, Baldy stopped pacing Pete to trot a few steps ahead and halt. The big dog bristled. Black nostrils twitched as he lifted his head to drink in a scent. He looked questioningly over his shoulder.

Pete took his rifle with both hands and laid his right thumb on the safety. He ordered softly, "Come back here, Baldy."

Baldy dropped back and Pete went on, more slowly now. Although game of all kinds was less plentiful nearer town, one could expect to meet wolves, grizzlies, and moose an hour out of Spruce Crossing. There was seldom any danger, however, for only on rare occasions did any wild thing attack a human. But, on the other hand, something *could*, so it was well to be ready. If the biggest and most dangerous beast, in the vilest of tempers, was lurking near and bent on trouble, there was little to fear, providing Pete saw it while he was still a reasonable distance from him. Three times he had stopped charging grizzlies with the rifle in his hands. He could stop anything else.

On a gentle but constant downward slope the trail from here on led through scrub aspens that had sprung up in the wake of a forest fire. Raging up the slope, the blaze had reduced all but a few once-stately spruces to charred stubs, with dead spikes of branches. Here and there, a green island in the scrub, stood an occasional spruce that had somehow escaped the conflagration.

Five minutes down the trail Pete found evidence of what Baldy had smelled. A hurricane that was not a hurricane at all, but a living creature of a mighty strength and evil intent, had descended on a twenty-yard square of the little aspens. Scattered branches, ripped from parent trunks, littered the earth and bore mute testimony to the fury that had raged among them. Broken boughs and trunks showed pitiful wounds, yellow and raw. Pete went forward and knelt to inspect the ground. He whistled.

Fury incarnate had been unleashed here. The track of the giant moose measured a full nine inches from pointed toe to dew claw. The size and weight of the mad creature were

made awesomely apparent by the impressions of its hoofs. Only a much more than normally big bull would have sunk in so deeply. Its sex could be instantly determined by the hoof-prints alone, all tracks toed out. Its capacity for destruction was evident in the wrecked aspens.

Pete rose and looked all about. He knew what he faced. The giant bull, searching for a mate and failing to find one, had obviously vented his insane frustration by attacking an entire forest. Doubtless he was a wanderer far from his own home, which could only be some secluded and seldom-visited wilderness area. A bull this size would be famous, if he were known at all. However, he was not necessarily dangerous. The biggest and strongest rutting bull was no match for a man with a rifle in his hands. Still, it was wise to be wary.

Pete wrinkled perplexed brows and looked down the trail. The scrub aspens were so thickly branched and so close together that their mass alone made it difficult to see clearly for more than a few yards and impossible to be certain of anything at all beyond a very limited range. It was a bad place, one to back out of or circle around under most circumstances, but the trail must be followed. To leave it meant to plunge into the snarl of brush and even more uncertainty.

Baldy whined and did an anxious little dance with his fore-paws. Their leader's nervousness spread to Jake and Megap, so that they crowded nearer to Pete and the safety represented in his rifle. Within themselves the dogs were a safety factor. Their very uneasiness told Pete that the bull was not far away, surely he was near enough to be scented. But he was not near enough to offer an immediate threat. The dogs would know—and they'd let Pete know—if he came too close.

Pete cut his speed in half and tightened his thumb pressure

on the safety. Eager anticipation more than fear guided both actions. The chances were greatly against the bull charging, but if the beast's antlers matched his body, he would be a rare trophy indeed. The hunter who brought him down would be entitled to another feather in his cap—and, besides, the Zluskis would welcome the meat. Casimir and Pete could pack it in with some of Casimir's horses.

A hundred or so yards ahead a slim-trunked spruce nodded its wind-ruffled head over the aspens, like a kindergarten teacher nodding over her pupils. There was no logical explanation as to why some of the spruces had survived the fire, but there appeared to be no doubt about this one. It stood on a little knoll where a rill crossed the trail and divided, to flow on either side of the knoll. The rill had checked the fire.

Pete halted and fixed his eyes on the treetop, even as he tried to control a sudden chill that rippled through him. He had an uncanny and momentarily terrifying thought that things were not at all as they seemed. The great bull knew all about him. Somewhere out in the scrub it was keeping silent pace, studying him with nose and ears and waiting for the proper moment to attack. . . . The idea was silly and Pete knew it! Moose do not hunt men. Just the same, he could not rid himself of the feeling until he forced his mind to cope with something earthly and feasible. Resolutely, Pete conjured up a mental image of the terrain immediately in front of him.

For the next fifty yards, approximately half the distance to the spruce, the trail wound a serpentine way through scrub aspens. Then there was a straight length from which the spruce's trunk was visible. Backed up by the knoll on which the spruce grew, the rill left a wide and shallow pool directly in the trail. However, there were steppingstones.

His confidence restored by coming to grips with and solving a practical problem, Pete resumed his slow advance. But, even though he told himself he was creating his own fears, he sighed with relief when he left the winding trail and came to the straight part. If the bull intended to attack, the winding trail, where clear visibility was restricted to four or five yards, would have been the ideal ambush. Although, even here, it was still impossible to see more than four or five yards to either side, the bull would never come so close without being detected by the dogs. More likely, he would first step into the trail, and, with fifty yards of clear shooting, he felt no qualms. He did not need that much to kill any moose.

Nevertheless, it was still wise to be careful. Rifle ready, not even glancing at the trail, Pete's eyes darted from side to side and ahead. He came to the pool, looked briefly down to make sure the steppingstones were as he remembered them, and leaped.

Just as he did so, Megap voiced a startled yelp and leaped, too. Baldy and Jake followed suit. To the cadence of Megap's continued yelping, all three animals raced full speed down the trail. Shoved by his own dogs, Pete flung out both arms to break his fall. His rifle probed deeply into the muddy pool.

Pete let the rifle go and, for a split second that somehow stretched into endless hours, he remained on all fours. He knew, but in a dazed and far-off way without any reality, that he should fear for his very life. The enormous black beast that floated out of the aspens was silent as a ghost, for all its bulk, but there was no mistaking its intent. Lip was lifted, mane bristled, and, as soon as it knew it was seen and silence was no longer useful, it began to grunt like an enraged pig.

It intended to kill him, but, in the first dazed instant, Pete

knew only that the situation was both embarrassing and ridiculous. He was being attacked by a gigantic moose, but he was not on his feet, defending himself with a rifle. Instead, he was on all fours, as though he, too, were a beast, and his rifle had fallen in the mud. Beyond question the bore was plugged. To shoot it without first cleaning it would be very dangerous. . . .

The dazed second passed but comprehension did not follow. Rather, there was an interval of complete blankness that made not the faintest mental impression. . . . Pete's awakening came when, from fifteen feet up in the spruce he had climbed unthinkingly with a forty-pound pack still on his shoulders, he turned to see the furious bull leap, strike with a sledge-hammer hoof, and miss his dangling foot by a hairbreadth. Awareness was followed by blazing fury.

"Blast you!" he snarled. "Blast you!"

The hatred that seethed within him was like nothing else he had ever known. He seemed to have been robbed of something very dear and precious, a vital part of his own self that he would regain only by killing this bull.

Nothing could ever be more important—but he could not do it now. A blow from his belt ax or a slash of his knife, always supposing he lived to deal either, could not harm such an enormous brute. His fingers ached for his rifle. Then a happy inspiration came.

The bull had backed off a few feet and was looking up. His eyes glowed with the same intense hatred that burned in Pete's. It was as though two foreordained enemies had finally met. Pete slipped the pack from his shoulders, but when he tried to hang it on a limb, he fumbled and dropped it. Without a glance for the pack, the bull kept his eyes on his captive.

Pete took his belt ax from its sheath, chopped a limb, pointed one end, and hurled his improvised spear at the bull. It struck the shoulder, causing not the smallest injury but rousing the brute to action. Lowering his antlers, he used his ton of muscle and bone and sinew to hurl them against the spruce. Head bent, neck muscles bulging, rear taut, legs braced, he strained to push the tree over.

He couldn't do it, but he could shake the trunk so violently that Pete was forced to cling with both hands. It was to be war and he expected no quarter—but when his turn came neither would he extend any! As soon as the bull backed away, Pete cut and hurled another wooden spear that brought another attack on the tree. Then, realizing the futility of anything he could do right now, Pete composed himself to wait things out.

He felt not the least resentment toward his dogs. In running away, they had not demonstrated storybook loyalty and a traditional willingness to die for their master, but they had at least shown rare good sense. There was really nothing they could have done if they'd tried to help. Three or thirty dogs couldn't hurt or even annoy this monster. Besides, in running, the dogs had served him much better than they would have if they'd remained.

Beyond any doubt, all three dogs would keep on running until they reached the Zluskis'. Pete Gant's dogs coming in without their master would tell their own story to Casimir and Hailey. The Zluskis certainly would search then. They knew he'd been in Spruce Crossing, so they'd come this way first. But there were no guarantees as to how soon they'd appear. At this season, both were busy herding sheep from summer pastures to winter range near their house and along the Wisbayah. Often, both spent the night with the flock. Unhappy thought!

Sundown brought a chill, and the twilight that followed shortly conveyed its own assurance that the Zluskis were not coming and Pete would spend all night in the tree. That is, he would unless the bull tired of what he was doing and went away. Then, startingly, the bull did go away.

First he was there and then he was gone, and Pete felt a different chill that was not born of the cold night air. Such an enormous brute should not be able to move as stealthily as a cat, but he had neither heard nor seen him leave. Still, he was gone. Pete waited another ten minutes, then cautiously descended the tree.

Instantly, he scrambled back up. There were a snort and a crackling of brush as the bull charged out of the aspens, where he had gone to hide. He hadn't left at all, but, with diabolical cunning, had tried to lure Pete within reach by making it appear that he was no longer interested.

Pete pulled his belt from its loops, slung it around a branch, buckled it, and clipped his arm through. He did not think he would sleep in the cold night, but if he should doze, he might fall out of the tree. That must not happen. Some time, of course, like every mortal creature, he would die. But not before he had a reckoning with the bull.

From time to time Pete glanced down to make sure the bull was still there. In the black night, he could never be sure, but it was wise to take no chances, and, even though he could not see the giant creature, he seemed to sense his presence. . . .

Dawn was faint in the sky when Pete finally dozed. . . . and the sun was shining whhen he jerked awake to see the bull, a drifting black shadow, slipping quietly through the aspens. A second later came Casimir Zluski's shout,

"Pete! Pete Gant! Are you around here?"

2

RUIN FOR CASIMIR

When Helen Zluski awakened, not a trace of daylight brightened the curtained window of her bedroom. A cold wind moaned about the eaves and plucked hopefully at the shingles. She lay very still and strained to hear. When there was no sound of her father moving about, she drew her heavy quilt up to her ears, turned on her side, and fixed her eyes on the window.

These very early mornings, before she must face any tasks the day brought, were precious indeed. In spite of darkness, she never saw more clearly or thought more sharply. As they usually did of late, her thoughts turned to Casimir.

Helen's personal memories began with this homestead. She'd been five when her father brought her here. Everything that had happened before this remained dark and murky, but all that came after was clear as the Wisbayah itself. This was far more than just a happy home. It was literally a place of resurrection, for here Casimir had come back from the dead.

Helen knew what half the men on the Wisbayah watershed

wished they knew and gossiped about and the other half considered none of their business. She knew her father's story.

Casimir Zluski looked sixty-nine years old, but he had just turned forty-nine. In his native Warsaw he had been an honored professor of economics but not by any means a pedagogue only. Banks and business houses throughout his country consulted him.

Helen was the youngest of four children. There had been another sister and two brothers. The family lived in a style commensurate with the father's position until war began. But the German Army was not even close to Warsaw when Casimir Zluski "died."

Like most others in the Polish city, the Zluskis were living nervously and at the same time trying to live quietly. They left their house only when it was absolutely necessary. Looters, hoodlums, and fifth columnists made the streets unsafe long before there was military action.

Night was the most dangerous time, but it was night when Helen developed a raging fever. Since the doctor would never dare come to her, Casimir Zluski decided to take his two-year-old to the doctor. Revolver in his pocket and baby daughter in his arms, the journey was without incident—but the home they'd left was a charnel house when they returned. The four who should have been safest there lay where they'd fallen when their throats had been slit. The house was looted.

It would have been futile to call the police. The few loyal policemen who had not already been killed or imprisoned by traitors were too busy organizing mass resistance to think of individuals. If Casimir Zluski pledged personal revenge, who was his enemy? It was unthinkable to ally himself with other desperate men and he neither went berserk nor insane. He

"died." Not that his physical self ceased functioning, but of all that had made him a man there lived just enough to recognize responsibility toward his one surviving child and to act accordingly.

The next three years were absorbed in an odyssey that took the refugees to half-a-dozen countries before it had ended here. Somehow, Casimir Zluski had obtained enough money to build a house, provide necessities for their new life, and buy some horses and a nucleus of breeding sheep.

It had puzzled Helen endlessly, as she learned her father's story, as to why the polished urbanite and educator should choose to spend the remainder of his life in such isolation. Now she knew the answer. No human could walk through the fires that had seared this man without paying the price. It cost some their sanity and some their health. It had cost Casimir his faith in man and God. He came to the Wisbayah with a heartfelt conviction that all humanity was evil, and that the farther he could stay from it, the less it would taint him. But although Casimir turned his back on God, God did not desert him.

It was as though his steps had been guided to the one place in the entire world where he might find his lost soul. No human being could live on the Wisbayah for very long and continue to consider man the supreme power. Everything about this wild land proclaimed that, at best, he was a puny creature. And as the evil in man seemed to be developed through privation and destitution, so bitterness and hatred seemed to take root most swiftly and flourish best in those cramped quarters where human beings must scramble for dregs. In this land of room and abundance, they blew away on the wind.

Thus Casimir Zluski came to his resurrection and lived again. Once more he was reconciled with his God and, if not with all humanity, at least with the people he found here. They were a different breed. Because they saw more of Pete Gant than anyone else, Helen found herself thinking of him as a standard for right conduct. It was impossible to imagine Pete slitting a baby's throat, murdering some helpless woman, or mouthing inflammatory inanities to further the interests of some power-mad lunatic. It was impossible to imagine Pete doing anything at all except turning furiously on anyone who flouted basic human decencies.

Thoughts of the young trapper kindled a mischievous gleam to mingle with affection in Helen's eyes. Pete was very kind, very good—and he was also a great lumbering bear who called her Hailey because he couldn't pronounce Hela. Not that there was anything offensive in such a nickname, somehow it matched Pete. She read him as easily as she might read a book, and knew, among other things, that he was secretly afraid of all girls and, at the same time, that he worried greatly about her. Because she appeared fragile, Pete thought she was. He always stayed overnight with them when he passed their way and he was always very welcome. But, much as she enjoyed his company, Helen could never resist teasing him. Her father sometimes scolded her gently for this, but Pete never seemed to mind.

Forgetting Pete, Helen's smile faded and she frowned in the early-morning darkness. Her father, who had known nothing of farming or sheep raising, had conquered this distinct handicap by dint of Herculean effort, applied intelligence, and self-denial. Although wool was harvested and sold at the proper season, the only sheep ever sold were those too old for breeding and surplus ram lambs. The flock had not yet provided a livelihood, but as long as there was money for staples, there was no need to worry. The summers were short, but the summer days were almost twenty-four hours long and vegetables flourished miraculously. In their season, wild berries of various kinds were there for the gathering. Although the Zluskis' table was never graced by conventional, butcher-shop cuts of meat, Helen had long since mastered the better ways to roast standing ribs of moose, broil venison steaks and chops, and get the tastiest effect from trout and grayling. The fat of bears was an admirable substitute for lard and bacon.

The reward was finally within reach. The four ewes and ram that Casimir Zluski had brought to the homestead thirteen years ago had become a flock of two hundred and fifty select sheep. This was not large as flocks go, but it should not be increased. Wool might be shipped from Spruce Crossing and

return a reasonable profit, but mutton could not be sold. At least in the foreseeable future, Casimir's only mutton market must necessarily be restricted to the Wisbayah watershed and the surplus from two hundred and fifty sheep would supply that. Obviously, their flock would never make them wealthy, but both Helen and her father would be entirely satisfied if they might continue to depend on their sheep for necessities—with perhaps a few luxuries.

Helen's frown intensified as she lay there in the darkness. Something aside from ordinary problems of day-to-day living had aged her father before his time. She suspected that the answer lay in those three years it had taken them to journey from Poland to the Wisbayah. But he seldom spoke of the journey and she never asked. There were more important matters to consider. If any misfortune whatever should wipe out all or a substantial part of their gains, would her father have either time enough or strength enough to begin again? If disaster were withheld, could he now find the peace and happiness he had earned? Or was it already too late?

Presently, and clearly, Helen heard the kitchen door open and shut behind whoever had entered. At the same instant the first exploring streak of gray morning slipped about her bedroom window and extended stealthy fingers to feel it. She rose, throwing back the quilt. Slowly, she put on her tough levis and wool shirt. They were the smallest she'd been able to buy and still they fitted her slender figure loosely. But they were more comfortable and practical than any other garb. Before stooping to catch up her tiny boots, she waited awhile longer.

Her father, who certainly knew that she was not nearly so fragile as she appeared, had definite ideas as to what was proper for a lady. Because it distressed him to see her chop wood, carry heavy burdens, or otherwise engage in what he considered strictly man's work, she refrained from doing anything at all of which she knew he did not approve—at least, she refrained while he was where he might see her.

Except in summer, when even the very early mornings were mild and occasionally even hot, she made a point of letting him get up first and build a fire in the massive range, so the kitchen would be pleasant when she entered it. This was not especially because she wanted matters that way, but he did.

On the other hand, her father not only never objected when she helped with the sheep, he actually depended on her assistance. A far more skilled shepherdess than he was a shepherd, something within her went out to the silly, bleating creatures that were so helpless and so in need of care. Casimir Zluski knew the technique of herding sheep, she combined technique with understanding. Perhaps because they knew that she was aware of their needs, the sheep responded to her coaxing, even when they stubbornly rebelled at her father's driving.

Helen looked happily forward to the coming day, for she liked to work with sheep at all times and particularly when trail driving was in order. Now she waited eagerly for Casimir to heat the range. Long experience had taught her to the split second exactly how much time he needed. At precisely the right moment, she entered the kitchen, where a lighted kerosene lamp cast flickering shadows on a far wall. She smoothed her rippling black hair and smiled.

"Good morning, Dad."

"Hela!" Casimir whirled toward her and returned her smile. "Was I so noisily clumsy that you must awaken, too?"

"Of course not," she answered briskly. "Now you just sit

down and take it easy. I'll have breakfast in a shake."

"I can make it," he offered. "The kettle's on."

Helen said serenely, "I'd rather you just sat down and rested."

Casimir seated himself and Helen hummed as she washed, using some of the warm water, then went to her work. Breakfast was a daily chore, but it was still another little intimacy that contributed to a good life. Her father built the fire each morning and never failed to offer to prepare the meal. But not for any known reason would he eat his own cooking if she was there to cook for him. She stirred pancake batter that had been set the night before and measured coffee into the pot. When the kettle started to sing, she filled the coffeepot and slid it onto a hot lid while she laid strips of bear's bacon on a griddle.

"We'll have a lovely day for it," she fairly sang.

"Yes."

She stole a quick glance at her father and turned away to hide the concern that flooded her eyes. It was enough that he had come back to life without expecting a concurrent rebirth of youthful vivacity, she told herself. He'd always been a little grim, and a faint sadness lingered, even in his smile. This apathy was a recent development. She feared it, but had forborn mentioning it because of an aversion to mingling in anyone else's personal affairs. She took a bold step now.

"If you aren't feeling well, Dad, why don't you stay here? Folly and I can bring the flock in."

He laughed, and when he did so he was once more the old Casimir Zluski. "Now, Hela, would you really leave your poor old father to wallow in his senility? Or is Folly's company more inspiring than mine?"

"Oh, Dad!" she scolded.

He laughed a second time. "I hope Folly doesn't decide we've forsaken him, just because we left him with the sheep while you and I came here to sleep in comfortable beds."

"Folly's too wise to suppose we'd forsake him," Helen said.

"I suppose that is something else you may tease Pete Gant about when he stops with us on his return from Spruce Crossing," her father observed wryly. "You have not forgotten that he is responsible for Folly's name?"

She replied, "I haven't forgotten. When Pete brought us the puppy, he said the frisky little thing was foolish, perhaps too foolish even to herd sheep."

"You never forget," he murmured. "Hela, do your thoughts turn to Pete very often?"

She looked at him in mild astonishment. "Of course. Pete's our closest friend."

Her father said, "That he is. I sometimes wonder, Hela, if I did not wrong you very greatly when I brought you here?"

"What on earth are you talking about?" she demanded.

"You," he answered. "You should be doing what other young girls are doing and having what they have. What I've given you is this."

"What more do I want?"

"One day you will want a husband," was her father's unexpected answer.

Helen could not stifle a peal of delighted laughter. She lifted the bacon onto a platter and expertly spilled pancake batter on the sputtering griddle. Still laughing, she went to her father, slid an arm around his neck, and kissed him.

"Stop worrying, Dad." She giggled. "I promise you won't end up with an old-maid daughter on your hands."

He smiled affectionately. "On that promise I will depend."

After they had breakfasted, Helen tidied the kitchen, while her father made his usual morning inspection of the premises. Before she was finished, he returned to pack the simple lunch she had fixed and the few necessary utensils.

All the chores done, Helen put on her light jacket, letting the hood dangle down her back so that the wind might play with her hair. Perhaps, she thought secretly, her father was not too greatly in error. Often, in her fancy, the wind was not the wind at all but a dream prince, caressing her hair. Then she made a face at herself for allowing such thoughts, caught up her little 32 Special, waited for Casimir to inspect and load his great 30-06 and shoulder the lunch pack, and set off beside him. There was plenty of meat on hand and probably no need for either rifle, but one could never be sure. This was grizzly country, and, although most grizzlies fled full speed at the sight of man, some didn't. Anyway, it was better to carry a rifle one didn't need than to leave it behind and need it!

They walked along in silence, for so perfectly were these two in tune with each other that words were not always necessary and, at times, they were even superfluous. This was their life, the one they had made for themselves, and neither even thought of any other. What they already had was far too dear to relinquish or to waste so much as a single moment of it.

The six horses, cropping grass in the meadow, looked up briefly as they passed, then resumed foraging. A cow moose with a half-grown calf beside her lingered near the forest, at the clearing's upper end. In a moment, Helen thought, she and her youngster will drift into hiding and they will do so as silently as two puffs of smoke. But although the pair did not venture any distance from the sheltering forest, they did not

fade into it. Casimir Zluski regarded his daughter with questioning eyes.

"That is unusual," he observed.

"Indeed it is," Helen agreed. "Why do you suppose they won't hide?"

He shrugged. "It seems to me that they are afraid."

"What could they fear?"

"Obviously not us," he replied. "At least not to the same degree that they fear something else. Perhaps we shall find out."

They took the spruce-bordered path that paralleled the

Wisbayah. On it the sheep traveled outward every summer and back to the homestead every winter. Helen noted with pleasure that, in distinct contrast with last year's low cycle, wild things were again climbing toward a peak population. Not that population peaks in the wilderness ever brought anything except mass tragedy. The increase mounted until there were too many living creatures for available food, then starvation or disease thinned their numbers and they must start all over again.

Still, one did not have to think in such a fashion, she told herself. One could concentrate, for example, on the thought that deer were as graceful as ever; the spruce hens as trusting; the great-footed hares that scooted out of or into every copse of brush as amusingly ungainly—and that the lynx and foxes would fare well during the winter to come. She sighed involuntarily.

Her father turned to face her. "So? Why not share your thoughts?"

"I was thinking of the delightful wild things," she told him, "But when I got around to considering snowshoe hares, I thought also that the lynx and foxes will fare well."

He nodded understandingly. "So it is. So it must be."

Theirs seemed a leisurely pace, but in a disappointingly short time the clearing around Raven Pond was seen through the trees. Such walks, Helen thought, should last forever. This one was already half finished and there remained only to drive the sheep down the trail. Then it occurred to her that sheep move very slowly and it would be impossible to reach home before dusk, anyway. Thus reassured that the day was all hers, she became eager for a sight of the flock. They entered the clearing—and both halted in their tracks. Helen gasped.

The clearing was a natural one that began on the east bank of Raven Pond and extended a quarter of a mile toward the forest. It was about a half mile long, and it was always the last clearing where the sheep were grazed before being brought in for the winter. A few yards from the pond was a little knoll on which a cluster of spruces grew. It was on this knoll that Folly usually lay or sat to watch his feeding flock. The high point offered a long view in all directions.

There was no Folly on the knoll now, and there were no sheep in the clearing except some that lay still as so many gray boulders. Too stunned to think, Helen followed the line of dead sheep with her eyes. She understood vaguely what had happened.

Having browsed their fill, the sheep had come in for water and bedded at the base of the knoll. Whatever had sneaked up on them in the night must have been a complete surprise, since the first huddle of the dead sheep had been slain in their beds. The rest had stampeded, but their swiftest speed was not fast enough. The killers had kept pace, pulling down the sheep as they ran and apparently wherever they chose.

Helen started counting the dead sheep—but stopped when the total mounted appallingly. She turned stricken eyes on her father and wondered numbly if he realized what he saw. With eleven years of hard work lying destroyed under his very eyes, she read neither anger nor despair in his face, but only an understanding pity.

"Come," he said softly.

She followed him to the base of the knoll and looked on dazedly as he knelt to read sign. . . . Finally he rose to face his daughter.

He said, "Wolves. The packs are beginning to gather."

She nodded numbly. A normal pack of timber wolves consisted of a mated pair and their cubs of the season, but when winter approached, one or several families would join to form a pack of twenty or more. Although sometimes they came so near that their mournful night howling was heard from the house, this was the first time they had molested the flock. Helen forced herself to speak.

"What now?"

Casimir shrugged, and there was just a trace of weariness in the gesture. "We must find if any escaped."

"But—but the wolves?" Helen whispered.

He answered gently, "One cannot hate wolves, Hela. At least they had a reason for killing. They wanted to eat. When they came across so many sheep so easy to kill, I suppose they found it impossible to stop. It is not unusal."

"I see." Helen moistened dry lips so she could speak clearly. "Lead on, Dad."

She followed her father along the line of pitiful gray markers, each of which had been a live sheep. A great anxiety gripped her as they neared the forest. She could not see into it . . . and perhaps the racing wolves had halted at the edge of the meadow. But the trail of slaughter ended only where the killers had finally stopped to gorge themselves.

When they reached the end of the massacre route, Helen knew dully that most of their sheep lay dead behind them but some few had escaped. With a sudden surge of hope, she remembered that she had not seen Folly among the many victims of the wolves. She offered a silent prayer for his safety.

A mile and a half beyond the last dead sheep they found the remnant of the flock at a tamarack swamp, where Folly had at last managed to regain control of his terrified charges.

There were fifty-two, including the great ram Vladimir. Combined physical and nervous exhaustion had reduced all to a point where they could do little except stare. Some were hurt, but only by accidents that had occurred during the stampede, for no sheep had ever felt a timber wolf's fangs and survived.

Silver-gray Folly, exhausted as his sheep but doing all he could to keep the survivors together, cringed forward on his belly when Helen and her father appeared.

Leaning her rifle against a tree, she ran forward to kneel beside the dog and fling both arms about him. "Don't blame yourself!" she cried. "You did all you could!"

"Yes." Until he spoke, Helen did not know that Casimir had come to stand beside her. "Folly did all anyone could and more than most would. Look not so stricken, Hela. This is not the worst thing."

Her numbness fading, Helen looked up wonderingly at the face of this man who could speak in sucha fashion after a happening so terrible. It seemed to her that this was the first time she had ever really seen her father—and all he meant and all he was. He had endured the hottest flames, and instead of consuming him, they had refined him. She felt a sudden surge of pride, and in that moment knew she must be worthy.

"What now?" she asked steadily.

Casimir replied, "Think first of our living sheep, Hela, and it will be a slow journey home, since some are hurt and all are weary. We must be all night on the trail."

"But—" Hailey started and could not go on. Her father understood and ansyered the unspoken question.

"We will try, and if anything may be saved, of course we shall save it. But it is better not to hope for much. The meat of the dead sheep will be hopelessly bloated by the time we may return and rest assured that the wolves, as well as other hungry creatures, will come here to feed while we are going down the trail. I doubt if many of the pelts will be worth taking. But think of good things, Hela. We still have a flock."

"Let's start," she said.

She strode toward the flock, and, as soon as he recognized his mistress, the curly horned Vladimir blatted happily and ran to her. One hand carrying her rifle and the other around Vladimir's neck, Helen started back toward the trail, the massive Vladimir walking willingly beside her. Folly and Casimir took their proper places at the rear as the lesser sheep fell in behind Helen and Vladimir. When a ewe fell and could not rise, Casimir caught her up and carried her. . . .

They made their first rest stop only a quarter of a mile from where they had started . . . and the next a little beyond that. The speed of the whole flock necessarily must be adjusted to that of its feeblest member. . . . They were not quite halfway down the trail by midnight. While Folly kept watch over his sheep, Casimir built a fire and brewed tea.

Gray dawn was faint in the sky when, driving only about a fifth of the sheep they should have brought, father and daughter came again to their homestead on the Wisbayah.

Helen wondered at herself, and why she could no longer regard this in its true light as a crushing tragedy. Somehow she seemed, at long last, to have either a whole new set of values or to have recognized old ones in their true light. There was tragedy, but never futility, and if the Zluskis were wiped out, they would build again. Then she saw Pete Gant's dogs clustered around the back door and called, "Dad, look. The back door!"

"*Hm-m*," Casimir pondered. "Pete Gant's dogs and still wearing packs. Come on!"

Leaving the weary sheep to feed and rest in their home pasture in care of the tired Folly, the pair ran forward. Pete's dogs stood quietly while Helen and her father unbuckled their harnesses and removed their burdens.

Casimir straightened and, turning to Helen, asked quietly, "Do you want to stay here, take care of these dogs, and make things ready for our return?"

She answered quickly, "I'd rather go with you. I may be able to help Pete and the dogs aren't suffering. They can wait a bit longer."

"Come on then. Pete would be on his way from Spruce Crossing."

Casimir set a swift pace up the trail heading toward Spruce Crossing and Helen hurried along behind him. Neither spoke, and for more than forty minutes Casimir did not even break his stride. . . .

Finally, he halted to shout, "Pete! Pete Gant! Are you around here?"

"Here!" came Pete's angry answer. "Watch yourself! The biggest moose in the world has had me treed all night and he's still on the prod!"

3

PETE MAKES A MOVE

HIGH IN THE SPRUCE Pete Gant looked over the surrounding scrub aspens and saw the Zluskis while they were a considerable distance down the trail. He grunted his annoyance, knowing his dogs had reached the Zluski house long before dark. Although they must have realized he was in trouble, Hailey and her father had still seen fit to wait for morning before starting out to find him!

They lacked even the lame excuse that they hadn't known where to look, for both knew he'd been in Spruce Crossing and that he would be coming from that direction. Pete told himself indignantly that it was a lot more comfortable to wait the night out in their house and start in the morning. Obviously they were not of the caliber he had thought they were. Any native of the back country would stop whatever he was doing to offer what he could to help anyone in distress, but evidently Casimir had been reared by a different code. In spite of his years on the Wisbayah, he was still alien. But at least, he, Pete, could finally come down from the tree.

He slipped his arm out of the looped belt and reached for a limb. His hand touched it, but he could not make his fingers grasp it. Nor were his feet anything except dead weights that responded only to concentrated and painful effort. After spending most of yesterday afternoon and all night in the spruce, he was stiff and cold-numbed. But if he broke both legs doing it, he'd climb down before the Zluskis arrived, Pete determined.

He stabbed at a limb, almost missed, found a precarious grip, then for a short space dangled while his body swung back and forth. Finally, his groping feet came to rest on a lower limb. Inch by inch he worked his way to the trunk, wrapped arms and legs around it, and climbed awkwardly down. He was still seven feet from the ground when he lost his hold and fell, to tumble over backward on the needle-carpeted ground.

Unhurt, but stiff as an arthritic octogenarian and still numb, he rolled over, rose to hands and knees, and crawled to the spruce. He clawed up its trunk, regained his feet, turned to brace his back against the tree, and brushed haphazardly at himself. At least, he thought grimly, he would be standing up and facing the Zluskis when they appeared. They would not find him in the spruce, as though he were some stupid, bark-nibbling porcupine.

A few minutes later, side by side and rifles ready, the two came. Hailey's dark eyes reflected sympathetic concern. Her father's, Pete thought savagely, held more than a hint of mirth. But Casimir's manner and voice were serious enough.

"What were you doing in the tree, Pete?" he asked gravely.

"Can't you guess?" Pete snapped. "Men are descended from

monkeys and every so often I have an urge to live as my ancestors did!"

"Oh!" Casimir's nod seemed to indicate that such an explanation was wholly within reason. He commented, "You look a bit stiff."

"You need glasses!" Pete growled. "I'm limber as a willow switch!"

"Oh, Pete!" Hailey scolded. "You needn't be angry! We came as quickly as we could!"

"Of course," Pete agreed. "Since my dogs couldn't have reached your place more than two or three hours before sundown yesterday, you must have run the whole distance!"

Casimir said gently, but with an undertone hard as flint, "Lay off Hela, Pete. What happened?"

"I was on my way to your place when–"

Pete stepped away from the spruce and immediately grabbed at his trousers. Casimir grinned broadly. Hailey stifled a giggle. Pete glanced up at the belt he had looped around a branch and forgotten to bring with him when he descended the spruce.

Hailey offered quickly, "I'll get it."

Handing her rifle to her father, she scooted up the spruce as though climbing were even less of an effort than walking. Reaching the belt, she seemed to balance lightly as a bird might as she loosened it and threw it down. Pete strung the strap through his trouser loops and buckled it.

At once, as though a man without his pants or one in danger of losing his pants somehow ceases to be a man at all, he felt different. Weariness evaporated–and numbness with it. Fury boiled to the white-hot point it had reached when the bull had chased him up the tree.

"I found moose sign up the trail and knew it was a rutting bull," he told Casimir. "Although I didn't expect trouble, I kept my eyes peeled anyway. I was about to cross the run when the dogs smelled the bull coming and bolted. They knocked me in. My rifle went deep in the mud and, of course, I didn't dare shoot it before I freed the bore. Then this bull—"

Suddenly, Pete was aware that Hailey had descended the spruce and was standing beside him. He hesitated. What he had to say was for Casimir alone. No child, especially a girl child, had any business listening in. Besides, she wouldn't understand what he was talking about if she did listen. But since Casimir made no move to dismiss Hailey and indicated in no way that she was out of place here, Pete continued, "I made it up the spruce just in time. When the moose reared and tried to knock me down, he missed by less than the width of a dog hair. That's about it, except that he's far and away the biggest bull I ever saw and I'll kill him if it's the last thing I do!"

He glared defiantly at the girl and saw that the mirth was gone from her eyes and a strange, haunting fear had replaced it. Casimir's face was no longer readable. Pete wondered. Both Hailey and her father not only killed moose, but they counted on filling their licenses as one source of meat for their table.

"Let's have it," Pete demanded.

"What?" Casimir asked.

"Whatever I said that rubbed your fur the wrong way. Is this your pet bull or something?"

"Sure, he's our house pet," answered Casimir shortly.

Hailey exclaimed, "Don't be silly, Pete!"

But the two were still looking at him and at each other, as though he had somehow managed to give deep offense to both. He had a sudden, wild notion that they had resented interrupting their own daily routine to come find him, and this was why they had waited for morning. "Wherever Pete Gant might be," he heard them saying, "he'll still be there when the sun rises. We might as well be comfortable tonight."

Pete turned his back on both and strode to the pool where he'd fallen. Mud stirred up by the panicky dogs had settled during the night, so that, once again, the water was clear. His rifle lay with the butt plate only an inch or so beneath the surface, but the barrel was buried to the forearm.

Stooping, Pete grasped the stock, wrenched his rifle out of the mud and held it at arm's length to let muddy water drip away. He had hoped to set out on the bull's trail as soon as he could, but his rifle needed a thorough cleaning, and perhaps some sight adjustment, before he would dare use it. Although Casimir and Hailey each had a rifle, he'd ask neither for the loan of theirs. He wanted no favors from anyone who'd let a man sit in a tree all night and then act miffed because he proposed to kill the bull that had kept him there! There'd still be another day and another meeting with the great bull, and he would be ready when that day came.

Casimir, who had been stooping to study the bull's tracks, straightened when Pete returned. He said seriously, "That's a mighty big moose, Pete."

"I told you it's the biggest I ever saw."

"This is not his home country," Casimir pronounced. "A moose that size would be known and marked. He came from elsewhere, maybe far from here, and only he knows why he left his stamping grounds."

"Did you figure that out all by yourself?" Pete asked sarcastically.

Hailey favored him with a sharply reproving glance, but

Casimir appeared not to notice. After that, neither father nor daughter spoke and neither made a move down the trail. They were, Pete knew—and somehow that added to his irritation—waiting for him to say that he was unhurt and ready to go. Reluctantly, he announced, "I'm all set if you are."

"Good!" Casimir nodded his shaggy head. "I expect you can use some breakfast."

Pete waited for the Zluskis to take the lead, then fell in behind them. Although he'd traveled this trail more times than he could remember, somehow it seemed that this was his first trip over it. Nor was anything else as it had been. A radical change had come into the Wisbayah Valley when the great bull invaded it.

There had been a time, Pete reminded himself, when he wouldn't have cared a summer-caught weasel pelt whether a man was born in Poland, Russia, or Iceland. Nor would his color, religion, or education mean anything. He had just found out how much real difference background can make. The Zluskis were *in* this country. They were not and never would be *of* it, and as aliens they must be measured.

Wagging happy tails, and roaring a discordant welcome, Pete's dogs met the trio just before they broke out of the forest. With an affectionate pat for Baldy and a word for Jake and Megap, Pete looked with wondering eyes at the little knot of sheep that grazed far down in the clearing and well away from the forest.

On his way to Spruce Crossing he'd stayed overnight, as usual, with the Zluskis. But he'd never been especially interested in Casimir's sheep and, at the time, he had not inquired about them. But he was very sure that there had been many more than this. Belatedly, he was also uncomfortably sure that he'd been rude and unreasonable. Casimir and Hailey had waited until morning to come find him, but it was anybody's guess as to how long he'd have been held captive in the spruce if they hadn't come at all. It was time to make amends.

He asked, "Has your flock been cut down, Casimir?"

Without looking over his shoulder, Casimir answered, "Yes, quite a bit."

Again, and for no discernible reason, there occurred the same cool withdrawal that had been so evident back at the spruce when Pete voiced his intention to kill the bull. Why, he wondered? Then Hailey pivoted to look at him with suddenly blazing eyes.

"The flock has indeed been cut!" she snapped. "We went to bring it in from Raven Pond and found that wolves had cut it for us! The sheep you see are all we have left and some of those are hurt! That's why we needed all night to bring them home and it also explains why we did not start out to look for you sooner! We did not find your dogs until we got in, and we got in just a couple of hours ago!"

"But–but–" Pete stammered. He felt suddenly and abjectly ashamed and he could not look into the flashing black eyes of this scornful girl.

Casimir spoke in the same gentle voice, but it was built on the same indestructible foundation he had used when warning Pete to stop exercising his sarcasm on Hailey. "Pete could not know that, Hela."

Hailey clapped a hand over her mouth and now her eyes reminded Pete of those of a wounded fawn. "Of course not! I'm sorry if I hurt your feelings!"

"It's–it's all right," Pete mumbled.

For a moment he wished desperately that this unpredictable

girl were ninety miles away and that he had a man, any man at all, beside him instead. You could always tell what a man was thinking and what he intended to do. But what could you tell about a girl who flared like a comet one second and was sweetness incarnate the next? He wondered suddenly, if the change he had sensed in all about him was centered in Hailey —then knew it just couldn't be. Nobody changed that much that soon.

When Pete and the Zluskis entered the house, Baldy, Jake, and Megap settled near the door. Now and again they looked wistfully toward the sheep. So many helpless creatures so near presented a mighty temptation. But no dog yielded. They were not afraid of Folly. Pete's dogs fought one another but always united against strangers. They did fear the lightning that would not fail to strike if they turned against anything protected by the invisible but omnipotent shield of human beings. Pete's dogs would not have molested the sheep if they were grazing all alone in some isolated wilderness meadow.

Casimir kindled a fire. While Hailey busied herself getting breakfast, Pete looked to his rifle. It was not so bad as it might be, he was relieved to find. A clean patch and a ramrod ejected most of the mud from the bore and succeeding patches finished the job. Gritty sand particles that had worked into the action yielded to a cloth soaked in kerosene. The stock and forearm were easy to clean. Although the sights seemed undamaged, Pete would have to shoot it *in* before he knew definitely. However, that was a simple job.

When Hailey announced breakfast, Pete stood his rifle in a corner and dawdled until Casimir had seated himself. Then he took his own place so that her father was between Hailey and himself. Not that he hadn't sat beside her many a time, and walked with her in the forest, and showed her how to lure bull trout with meat scraps, and even pushed her on her swing when she was much younger—and all of it with never a second thought. But he would not do these things in exactly the same way ever again.

With a very rare and very dazzling flash of insight, Pete knew that the world had not changed—but Hailey had. Even though she looked the same, acted the same, and talked as she'd always talked, she was entirely different. It was not a trait she had always had and that somehow had escaped Pete's notice until now. Nobody could fail to notice anything so startling.

Pete could neither identify nor understand it, therefore he was a little afraid of it. His preoccupation induced a moody silence.

"Did that bull scare you clear out of talking with us?" Hailey teased.

Pete started, then grinned. "Could be."

Now that his thoughts had been diverted to the bull, a creature he understood to the minutest detail, he felt easier. If he no longer nourished the blazing fury that had colored his cheeks while the bull snorted beneath him, what he did feel was deeper rooted and enduring. It was as much a part of him as his right arm, and he could no more be rid of it than he could cut off that arm. It would go of its own accord when he killed the bull, but it would let him have no peace until he did.

Casimir asked, "Why not lay over a couple of days, Pete? We never have so much company that we couldn't use more."

Pete found himself answering, "I've been thinking about moving right in with you, Casimir. Fur's none too plentiful back on the lakes this season, but from the sign I've seen, there's plenty here."

Haileys' eyes glowed, and Pete wondered at the sudden joy that danced within them. Surely it was not for him. Hailey was always glad when he came, but she was equally happy when anyone else came. As Casimir had said, company was always welcome in this place where so very little of it appeared.

But something had lifted Hailey above mere happiness to near ecstasy. Pete could not even guess that her deepest wish was on the point of coming true. A normal and healthy man has nothing to fear in the wilderness, but gradually, she had become convinced that Casimir was no longer healthy or normal. To have someone nearby, someone who would help her if help were needed and whom she could reach quickly, might mean the difference between her father's salvation and his destruction.

"There is a lot," Casimir agreed. "This seems to be a peak year."

"Dad's right, Pete!" Hailey exclaimed. "You'll do much better here than you will back on the lakes!"

Pete centered his thoughts on the great bull. He might have wandered once, but he had found a satisfactory homeland now and the chances were a hundred to one he'd stay in it.

"You needn't build more than out cabins if you come here," Casimir said. "Make this your headquarters. Hela and I will be delighted to have you."

Pete brought his fist down on the table. "I'll take you up on that, Casimir!"

At the same instant, Hailey's delight gave way to a sudden chill and a rising fear. She twisted uncomfortably, feeling that something ugly and unwholesome was about to come into her life and her father's. It would be a godsend to have someone strong near, but, with almost unreal clarity, she saw again Pete's eyes when he spoke of his intention to kill the bull, and her flesh crawled. In the same instant, she knew that it was the bull, and not the prospect of more fur, that was bringing the young trapper to the Wisbayah.

She told herself that she was familiar with death. Life itself could not be without death. But death should have, not merely a purpose, but a lofty purpose, and that made it noble. If it were brought about through senseless hatred, such as that which inflamed Pete Gant's brain, it was evil. She laughed lightly to mask her own distress.

"You should really think twice about coming," she said.

"You'll do as well, and perhaps a great deal better, back on the lakes."

"Hela!" the shocked Casimir reproved.

Pete said with feigned sorrow, "Hailey doesn't like me any more!"

"Of course I like you," Hailey soothed–and wished she knew a gracious way to add, "as you were, but not as you are."

Pete and Casimir immediately became involved in a discussion that concerned the most practical way for Pete to move. There were endless details, most of which were rooted in the fact that backwoods trappers, even wilderness trappers, know all about the march of progress and do their best to keep pace with it. Pete's out cabins were no more than rude shelters, for their only purpose was to furnish an overnight protection when he ran long trap lines and was unable to return to his base camp. The latter, however, offered every comfort and convenience that can be fastened on a pack saddle. If a horse can carry it, an experienced packer can transport anything anywhere a horse can walk. Heavy articles are taken apart, packed on several horses, and assembled at the point of destination. Pete's base camp boasted a modern kitchen range, a potbellied heating stove, an innerspring mattress, an assortment of books, which included a twenty-volume encyclopedia, and other articles of a similar nature.

"The season's getting on," Pete told Casimir, "but I can make it all right if I shake myself. I'll leave what's already here and kite on up the trail."

"Of course you'll take my horses," Casimir suggested.

"I'd better, if you don't mind," Pete said. "But since I'll base here with you and Hailey, I'll leave my stoves and such there. I don't want to abandon Two Moose, and I'd just as soon not bring all that heavy gear down, then pack it back up again."

"Good idea," Casimir commented. "You needn't bring the stoves from your out cabins, either. I have a lot of oil drums in the shed. Just cut a door and a stovepipe hole and you've got a stove. I can even lend you the stovepipe. How about taking me along to give a hand?"

"Thank's, Casimir, but there won't be that much to do if I leave the heavy stuff. A couple of trips will swing it."

Hailey sprang up. "I'll bring the horses."

Driving Casimir's six horses, with Baldy beside him and Jake and Megap in the rear, Pete started up the trail. He stopped just before he entered the forest to turn and wave a farewell. Casimir and Hailey waved back to wish him God-speed.

4

THE OUT CABIN

THE Zluski homestead offered access to a ford, one of a very few where the Wisbayah might be safely crossed at any time, except in flood waters. But most of the people who came this way intended to stay awhile and brought considerable gear. This presented no problem to those with pack horses. But those with none faced the uninviting prospect of backpacking everything—always a matter of several trips—and wading across the icy river. Dogs could carry only those things that would not be harmed by water, since whatever they packed never failed to get soaked.

Casimir had built a boat for his own use but he had also made it available to all travelers. It was a sixteen-foot scow, designed to carry a maximum pay load and at the same time retain maximum maneuverability. Although it was no canoe, the loaded scow drew only a few inches of water and was practically incapable of capsizing. Oar-propelled, it was also equipped with a rudder that made any downstream journey a positive luxury, since the traveler needed only loll on the back seat and stear. A line could be strung from the scow to the bank, so coming back up presented no problem, if one had dogs to do the towing. The unlucky upstream traveler who had no dogs might just as well get out and pull the scow himself, because that was easier than rowing a blunt-ended boat against the current.

Travelers bound for the far side of the river were rowed across by Casimir or Hailey, and the scow was then returned to its landing. Travelers coming from the far side must attract attention by yelling, shooting their rifles in the air, or any other way that occurred to them, and the scow was brought over. When both Hailey and Casimir were absent, travelers from the far side had a choice of waiting until they returned or tackling the ford. Most chose to wait.

Going downstream a short time after he had transferred his needed equipment from Two Moose, Pete Gant thought with satisfaction that he faced nothing more strenuous than keeping one hand on the tiller, at least for the present. Baldy, Jake, and Megap were up front. Pete had brought harnesses for all three dogs, as well as a towing rope. The remainder of his gear, including an empty oil drum in which he had already cut a door and a stovepipe hole, was distributed about the boat to make a trim load. Not that undue caution was necessary. Casimir had designed his scow to carry any load in any water. But a man who got in the habit of packing things right found it almost impossible to pack them wrong.

Pete swerved to glide past an upthrust rock and the white water that snarled on either side of it. A nagging uncertainty that of late was never absent, but sometimes lay dormant, flared suddenly.

It had been a good idea to transfer all operations to the Wisbayah this season. For one thing, it saved making the long trip from his camp on Two Moose so he could hunt down and kill the great bull that had treed him. Although it was anyone's guess as to why the bull had left his old home, there was no doubt that he found the new one to his liking and intended to stay in it. Pete and Casimir had each found his tracks and Hailey thought she'd seen him once. She could not be sure, however, since all she'd had was one glimpse as he faded out of sight in the evergreens and the rocky ground retained no tracks.

For another thing, this season, fur was far more plentiful in the valley of the Wisbayah than back in the lake country. It was a phenomenon Pete could not explain, and, to the best of his knowledge, neither could anyone else. It was comparable to the so-called rabbit famine, when all the rabbits supposedly died or disappeared and actually did no such thing. Even though a hunting weasel found it impossible to run across a single snowshoe, or even a single track, in an area where they had been thick as mosquitoes in June, there could be as many as ever no more than ten miles away. For reasons only they could explain, there were times when everything from rabbits to moose decided to pack up and move, and that was why game could be scarce in one place but overrunning another. Doubtless that explained the huge bull's presence on the Wisbayah.

In spite of the promising outlook, however, Pete was no longer sure as to the wisdom of making his headquarters with the Zluskis. Not that either of them had said or done anything to indicate he was unwanted or unwelcome–after all, Hailey had always had a tart tongue. But a feeling that was born in Pete the morning the Zluskis came up the trail to rescue him from the tree not only lingered but had become strengthened. Over the years, he thought he had grown to know Hailey—and, suddenly, he didn't know her at all. Once he'd held her hand protectingly while they waded, but that was a little girl he'd known. This Hailey was such a grown-up stranger most of the time that he felt as though they lived miles apart and he couldn't even reach her when he spoke!

It was difficult to believe she hated him—but, on the whole, it would be easier if she did. Hatred was a basic thing, a fundamental quality he could understand. Hailey seemed to shrink from him as she might shrink from some crawling, slimy creature that was equally disgusting to the touch or the eyes. Come to think of it, her father hadn't exactly fallen all over himself to be friendly, either. But Casimir had always been a bit aloof and how could you blame a man for acting as nature made him?

Well, unless he cared to pack everything back up to Two Moose, a big enough job, even though he had brought only his traps, food, and essential gear, it was too late to change again. He'd just have to carry his weight at the Zluskis and go on according to plan. If the air at the house got too thick, he'd hole up at an out cabin until it cleared.

Suddenly, there was motion on the right bank, a mere hint of black that melted instantly into the spruces. Pete dropped the tiller and leaped to the oarsman's seat. With long, powerful strokes that raised a miniature curl of water on either side of the scow, he rowed to the bank and grounded his boat. Then he caught up his rifle and stood.

Baldy and Jake blinked questioningly at him, but waited for his orders. When Megap would have risen, Pete, who

dared not risk alarming his game by talking, raised a hand as though intending to cuff him. Megap sank down beside Baldy and Jake.

Pete stopped ashore and went into the spruces. All he knew was that he'd glimpsed a moose. . . . He could not stifle a small disappointment when the track he found proved that he'd seen a cow. Then he grinned mirthlessly. It might have been the great bull and he intended to overlook no chance to kill him. It would not be easy to get a shot, or even get near him, except in the rutting season. It was a foregone conclusion that anything so big got that way largely because he was too smart for the various enemies that would like to kill him. But get him Pete would, if it meant tracking down every moose in the Wisbayah Valley first—and he'd kill him wherever he was found!

That, of course, meant a drastic deviation from usual and accepted practice around these parts. Any man who made his living in the wild country did well if he left trophy hunting to those who had other means of gaining a living and thought only of his table whenever he hunted. There was a lot of meat on any moose. Whoever killed one any considerable distance from where he intended to consume it must either leave a lot of it for scavengers or tackle a man-sized packing job. But if a man awaited his chances, sooner or later, he dropped his table meat within easy reach of that table. Hailey and Casimir Zluski always killed their moose when they came to feed on the hay stacked up for the sheep.

Pete floated the scow, took his place on the back seat, and resumed his journey down-river. Just before one o'clock he beached his craft where a wandering stream poured out of the hills into the Wisbayah. He nodded at the anxious dogs.

"All right. Come on."

They sprang up and ashore in almost the same motion, glad to leave the scow and be about their everlasting business—when they weren't working for Pete—of hunting snowshoe rabbits. Although they never caught any, that seemed immaterial. They not only tried again at the earliest opportunity but they spent all their free time hunting snowshoes. From a dog's point of view, Pete reflected, it must be a fascinating business. There was no need to worry about the trio. They'd come back when they got hungry.

Pete glanced up the river, and, as he was swinging to look down it, he saw a snowshoe crouching beneath a bushy spruce.

The dogs had passed within a dozen feet and never detected it, which was not unusual, considering that all three were work animals whose strength was far more important than their power of scent. The snowshoe held perfectly still, with long ears resting on its shoulders. It was so sleek that every hair seemed combed in place, but here and there its brown pelage was streaked with white.

Pete nodded soberly. It was indeed time for action. When the snowshoes traded their all-brown summer coats for their all-white winter robes, fur was prime for trapping, and a good catch early in the season could mean the difference between a fat check from a fur buyer and starting next season with a borrowed grubstake. Pete reviewed his plans.

He'd launched the scow shortly before eight o'clock and now it lacked just a few minutes to one. If he took a direct course–the river bent and twisted–it would be about ten miles to the Zluski house. While that was no formidable journey under most conditions, there was a lot of trapping in it. He'd take in all the streams, of course, and the river, too. Following the erratic pattern of a trap line and driving a dog team–since there'd soon be ice on the Wisbayah–he'd have to leave the Zluskis long before daybreak to come this far by night. Even so, he'd probably have to carry any trapped fur along with him and pelt it at the cabin. There wouldn't be time to do it along the way.

For a brief interval he wondered whether he was trying too much, then decided he could make it. He'd always had one long line and he'd let this be his long one on the Wisbayah, for he had a hunch the great bull had moved down-river and the more territory he covered, the better his chance of running across the beast. Coming down, in addition to hunting the bull, he'd trap the aquatic mink and otter, plus all other fur animals that visit streams. Going back, he'd swing into the hills and through thickets for fox, wolf, marten, fisher, ermine, and lynx, with emphasis on the latter–prime lynx always.

Pete started at a sudden and almost weird sensation that somehow someone else had just stolen full control of his thoughts. He remembered clearly that he had been on the point of thinking that prime lynx command high prices. But he found himself conjuring up a vision of Hailey Zluski wearing a lynx-trimmed cape. With a little shudder, he leaned his rifle against a tree and took his ax from the scow. Hard work always diverted his thoughts from anything he didn't want to think about.

Since he intended to build only an out cabin here, he could dispense with all frills. He chose spruces big enough to make a wall that would stand against heavy winds but small enough so that he himself could handle them easily, and trimmed and cut them to length as they fell. The branches were thrown to one side, all on the same pile, for later use as kindling. The trunks were arranged in a separate pile, alternating butt and tip ends.

Stopping only often enough to keep a razor edge on his ax, Pete was mildly surprised when long shadows and an evening chill heralded the day's end. But he was overcome with astonishment when he looked toward his pile of trunks. Remembering that he worked hardest when he wanted to put some particular subject from his thoughts, he grinned sheepishly. Hailey Zluski might be a smart aleck grown too big for her rightful place, but she wasn't *that* bad. Pete murmured an apology. "I'm sorry, Hailey. I'll make up for it by working real slow tomorrow and thinking about you every second."

Pete spread his sleeping bag and built a fire, but left it unlighted while he went down to the river with a casting rod. A genuine pleasure tingled through him. He did not share the opinion held by most wilderness trappers, that sport is fine for those who can afford and have time for it but trappers who hope to get along must think first of utility. He differed from these others insofar as he liked to take fish in a sporting way. Most trappers cut a stiff pole, attached a hank of line strong enough to picket a mule, baited with a chunk of raw moose meat, and heaved fish out as fast as they'd strike. Pete preferred a more refined angling.

He cast, and a dozen different ripples that converged on the lure from a dozen different directions offered their own convincing testimony that these waters were rarely, if ever, fished. Pete played a two-pound trout in to the bank and cast again. The next fish, a small one, he released. Then he kept two, freed another, and ended in a rousing battle with a six-and-a-half-pound trout that fought right up to the second he stooped to lift it clear of the water.

The weary dogs straggled in twenty minutes later. Pete threw a trout to each, wondering as he did so if the tales he'd heard were really true and if gourmets in distant cities gladly paid the price of a good mink pelt for such a dinner. True or not, his dogs had to eat, and they'd eat trout as long as it was the easiest thing to get.

Fortunately, he could satsify himself with whatever he needed for the moment. He'd caught and salted a plentiful supply of trout and grayling soon after the spring breakup. Salted fish were supposed to be better for dogs anyhow, and a quick grin lighted Pete's face as he recalled one old trapper's explanation as to why they were preferable.

"Shore they're better!" the querulous old-timer had asserted. "An' the more salt the better they are! Give a dog a reasonable good-sized fish without salt an' has he et anything? Nope! But give him a little fish with a heap of salt an' what's he do? He drinks up a gallon or so of water an' anyhow *thinks* he's et a big meal!"

Pete finished eating, threw the scraps to Baldy, and stared into the fire. Then, as though it had suddenly become a vital job that must be done at once, he threw an armful of fresh wood on it. As flames leaped and sparks floated upward, he tilted his head and looked into a tall spruce that stood near.

He had already decided that the spruce was the proper place to build his cache, a storage place where food might be kept safe from wolverines, marten, fisher, and similar prowlers with a talent for climbing trees and an inclination for piracy. If he put enough wood on, perhaps the fire would cast enough light to let him work on the cache tonight. But the fire did not throw that much light, and Pete turned mournfully away from the spruce.

Now that he had no work to do, there was no way in the world to keep his mind from picturing for him the unwanted image of Hailey Zluski.

5

ULTIMATUM

As he sometimes did when involved in a challenging mental problem, Casimir Zluski got up hours before daybreak, made his own breakfast, and retired to his study.

Hailey rose shortly afterward. The kitchen chores finished, she encircled the calendar date, the ninth of November, with a red crayon, for this was to be another red-letter day. As soon as it was light enough to see, she took her rifle and started for the woods. She had no intention of shooting anything and there was one chance in a thousand that she'd have to defend herself, but if that thousandth chance came up, it was well to be ready.

Folly, never bred as a sheep dog but with an acquired devotion to herding, greeted her with wagging tail as she passed but stayed with the sheep. Although he'd tried his best, Folly had been unable to grapple with even one of the freebooting wolves that had massacred four-fifths of the flock, and that was just as well for him. Few dogs are a match for a timber wolf. But Folly had every intention of being in a position to close with the next raider, and if his mistress wanted to ruffle his ears, she'd just have to come to him.

The foraging horses raised their heads and nickered softly as Hailey crossed the clearing and went on into the forest. With Pete absent on his trap line and her father absorbed in his books, nobody was likely to need her, so, for this whole, delightful day, she could belong to herself alone. She intended to spend it in a world that was also her exclusive property.

The green-needled spruces became a magic curtain that opened to let her in but closed at once to keep everyone else out. If one knew how, it was just that easy to step into a different world, so exclusive that it never would be revealed to any eyes except hers.

Hailey smiled at her own fancy but made no effort to direct her thoughts elsewhere. The entire charm of these free days rested on the fact that they became whatever she chose to make them. All she held dear was easily stripped of minor flaws and grew more precious as it became perfect. That which annoyed her was easy to exclude, unless she chose to let it come in. If she did, it must conform to her wishes and therefore it no longer annoyed.

The fairyland in which Hailey lost herself at periodic intervals was so intimately personal that not even Casimir Zluski knew where his daughter really went on her solitary rambles. But for some reason, the magic formula that had always been flawless for her revealed a fault today. Although her strictest rule provided that nothing could come into her private world without her permission, somehow she could not keep Pete Gant out.

It seemed that she was helpless to exclude him from anything. As an occasional visitor, Pete had provided a refreshing change. As a permanent guest, at best he was an awkward interloper, and at worst thoroughly repulsive. Hailey had had no genuine appreciation of her own and Casimir's way of life until she was forced to share it with someone who did not sympathize with it—or even understand it.

It was not, she told herself, that Pete was worse than other woodsmen—but neither was he better. It had needed the incident of the great bull to make that clear. Hailey still shuddered when she recalled Pete's eyes as they had been when he asserted that he would have revenge, and she could rouse herself to fury when she considered the stupidity of such a notion. A moose, a wild animal, had made Pete climb a tree and would not let him come down, so now Pete hated the moose.

Hailey saw this as a cardinal sin. Her mother, her sister, and her brothers were among the millions who were dead because someone hated. The same hatred had made an old man of her father long before his time. That such destructive emotion existed anywhere was a horror. How was it even being tolerated in the same house with her father and herself?

However, considering that her father had invited Pete to stay with them, even if she could bring herself to do such a thing, it was not for her to suggest that it would be as well if he went elsewhere. It was still her father's house. Hailey broke into a fast walk that speedily became a fast run. Before long, sighing resignedly, she dropped back to her starting pace. She could neither keep Pete out nor outdistance him, now that he was in—but at least she could keep him at arm's length.

Presently, she felt a sharp irritation, which couldn't possibly be directed at anyone except herself, because her invisible companion not only seemed happy to stay so far from her but would be even happier if he were farther away. Hailey forsook her private world to return for a moment to the one she shared with others. For no reason at all, she told herself, she was being silly. How could she expect Pete Gant to be on the same plane as her father? Very few men climbed to that high level, and if Pete's determination to have revenge on the bull was a childish trait, was he other than childish? Moreover, apart from the fact that it troubled both her father and herself, was the whole thing any of her business? Pete had come to their house and, in the course of time, he would leave. Meanwhile, in spite of new and troublesome problems, life was not intolerable and Pete was not without his good points.

He was surely an unsurpassed outdoorsman and trapper. Even though he'd had his traps in active operation less than a week, the fur stretchers in an out shed already held as much prime fur as her father had ever taken throughout a whole season. Nor, although he was jubilant and freely forecast his richest catch of any year, was he boastful. He freely admitted that it was an unusual catch, made possible only by an unusual abundance. According to Pete, any trapper lucky enough to be in the Wisbayah Valley this year just couldn't help sharing a bonanza.

Hailey thought with a sharp little pang of the wistful look on her father's face when Pete talked so. After eleven years on the Wisbayah, Casimir Zluski had only that which he had earned through his own hard work, and a great share of that had fallen to the wolf pack. Now that there was wealth for the trapping, he must sit by and see another man benefit. The very fact that he had set no traps and was spending more time in his study was its own admission that he did not feel equal to the grueling labor a trap line demands.

Hailey remembered Pete as he had looked the last time she saw him. Seated with his hand on the tiller, shouting brisk commands to the three harnessed dogs on the tow line, he'd gone upriver early yesterday morning and probably would come back down late today. He was making the most of open water while it laster, and judging by the nippy wind, that wouldn't be long. Therefore Pete must resort to packing, unless snow came with the freeze-up and enabled him to use a sled. Whatever the weather and regardless of his mode of travel, Pete would get there, and Hailey found the thought not entirely consoling. Pete would be easier to like if he were not so aggravatingly efficient. Everyone should not only need somebody else, but he should never hesitate to reveal such a need.

Sitting down on a fallen tree and balancing her rifle across her knees, Hailey slipped back into her own world and, this time, there was no intruder. Pete had been left up the river. She watched a snowshoe, its white coat glaringly obvious against the somber background, hop cautiously to a bush and start nibbling.

Pity moved her heart and righteous indignation her mind. The snowshoe, guilty of nothing more than blind faith, had trustingly changed from summer brown to winter white when cold weather indicated that such a change was in order. He was not responsible because no snows had fallen, and until they fell, he would not only be unable to camouflage himself but nothing with eyes could help seeing him.

Hailey could reverse such a violation of justice and did so at once. A single wave of her magic wand changed the snowshoe back to summer brown and assured him that he would not again be white until snow fell. Amused by her own fancy,

but intrigued with the game she was playing, for a moment she watched the snowshoe as though it really might turn brown. Then she raised her eyes and froze in startled immobility.

Down-wind, no more than a hundred and fifty feet away, a bull moose appeared. Her first glance told Hailey that it was not only big, but far and away the biggest she'd ever seen. The next instant she knew it was the bull that had treed Pete. Just in time, she stifled a chuckle.

She knew of the rut and the ferocity it aroused, but the rut was past now and the mating lust with it. Rather than the embodiment of fury, the bull reminded her of nothing so much as some placid old barnyard cow. Having already shed one antler, his head was grotesquely misshapen and tilted by the weight of the antler he still carried.

Hailey tried to visualize the moose she was looking at chasing Pete Gant up a tree and found it almost impossible to restrain her laughter. Her day in her private world, she gloated, had brought unhoped-for dividends. She knew something Pete Gant would give his winter's catch to know, but the secret would remain hers. Even if she found the shed antler, a prize worth having, she'd leave it rather than drop even a faint hint that she knew where to find the bull.

The big bull, walked down a fair-sized aspen, bending the top before him as he advanced. He held it between enormous legs while he nibbled tender shoots and chewed them with jaw-wagging gusto. Hailey watched with mounting glee as he walked on over the aspen and let it spring back into place. The very fact that she knew something Pete yearned to know somehow gave her an advantage over him and let her see him in a softer light. After all, he was not perfect. If he was, he'd have found the bull himself!

Hailey thought suddenly, and soberly, that just seeing such a creature was a rare privilege. There was no knowing where the big bull had come from or why he was here, but there was no doubting that his arrival forecast a drastic change in the lives of all moose of the entire area. No ordinary bull could possibly hold his own against such a beast, which meant that this great creature would have the cows of his choice. This, in logical sequence, almost certainly meant that future years would find an abundance of big bulls.

The great bull was in truth a living monument to the unalterable conception that no life is without meaning and death must never be without purpose—otherwise it is a sin, and whoever brings it about heedlessly must necessarily be a sinner. Thousands who had killed for personal gain, or revenge, or hatred, paid a price more dreadful than they extracted from their richest victim. If their punishment did not start while they were still on earth, not one among them could avoid the final reckoning.

Hailey sat very still while the big bull walked on . . . and she remained seated for forty-five minutes after he disappeared. He'd neither seen nor scented her, and his casual manner indicated that he felt sure of his safety on this new range he'd chosen. But he might leave if he thought he was discovered—and if he left he was apt to go where Pete Gant would run across him. When she was sure there was no longer any chance of frightening the bull, Hailey rose and started home.

Folly, as he always did when the shadows grew long, had brought his flock nearer the house and the protection therein, and the horses had grazed nearer of their own accord. But Pete had not come back down the river and Casimir was still in his study. He looked up, nodded, and smiled absently when Hailey paused briefly in the doorway. She smiled back and left him alone.

When her father concentrated on any project, he never had a passing thought for anything else. Obviously, it had not occurred to him to eat lunch and probably he knew only vaguely that the day was nearly spent or that Hailey had been absent.

He'd revert back to normal when called for supper and there was no point in disturbing him sooner.

Hailey built a fire and set about preparing the evening meal. It was a routine task that needed little thought, but never before had she been so wholly detached from what she was doing. A pulsing eagerness throbbed within her, so that she could not keep her feet from dancing or her body from throbbing to the same rhythm. She was suddenly eager to face Pete. Even though she would not tell him she had found the bull, her triumph would be incomplete until he returned and she might tell him. . . .

The day had given way to twilight when Folly's challenging bark announced Pete's return. Hailey put on her jacket and left it unbuttoned as she ran down to the landing. The scow glided in smoothly. Pete's dogs scrambled ashore and the young trapper followed. He stooped to pull the scow up, then turned to grin at her.

"Got here," he announced cheerfully.

"Of course," she said. "I knew you would."

She tried to speak in a very composed and matter-of-fact voice, but proved unequal to the task.

Pete looked searchingly at her. "What's up, Hailey?"

"I–I–" she surrendered to confusion. "I just wondered if you found that big bull?"

"I didn't," he said, "but I will. Someday I'll make you a present of his head."

"Is that all you can think of?" she demanded angrily. "Is that all you want to do?"

"Not all." For a discernible interval he seemed to deliberate. Then he continued, "There's something else I've had in mind."

Suddenly—and she hadn't the faintest notion of how she got there—she was in his arms and he was kissing her. She should never permit such a thing, she told herself, and she should resist it fiercely. But, instead of fighting back, she found herself kissing back. He released her abruptly and stepped away.

"There," he said shakily. "That's—that's what I had in mind. I'll leave now if you want me to."

For a moment she said nothing. Finally, she said in low tones, "You needn't leave, Pete, not for that." Then her voice gained unexpected firmness and her eyes flashed as she issued her ultimatum. "But don't you ever kill that big bull, not any time or for any reason. If you do, I don't want you ever to come near me again. Do you understand?"

Pete Gant retorted angrily, "I understand, but do you? I said I'd kill that bull and I aim to do it!"

Hailey gazed at him for a moment helplessly—almost pleadingly—then she whirled about and ran for the cabin.

6

THE TRIAL OF PETE

ALTHOUGH it lacked a half-hour to noon and there was plenty of time, Pete Gant floated past the last two tributary streams in which he had traps without turning aside. Clouds that were gathering when he left the Zluskis' before dawn had mustered in a scowling black curtain that shut out the sun and draped midday in the wan light of early evening. The wind, that had blown coldly and sharply from the north for ten days, shifted to the west and lost its bite. It was so warm that Pete let his parka hang open, with the cape thrown back, and the three dogs panted gently.

Following a prolonged period of freakish weather, all signs indicated a return to normalcy. The ominous clouds and the sudden warmth were positive assurance that the long-delayed snow would fall at last. The freeze-up was certain to follow. Baldy whined and turned to look toward his master. Pete grinned back at the dog.

"The honeymoon's about over, Baldy. From now on, we'll work coming and going."

It was not an uninviting prospect, in spite of the fact that a delayed freeze-up was partly responsible for an extraordinary early catch of fur. It was easier to trap mink and otter in open water than under the ice, but less interesting because it called for greater skill to take the nimble animals under the ice. Unusual things could happen, too. Pete remembered an incident from a couple of seasons past.

He always located his under-ice sets before freeze-up, and he had planted a mink trap in a dirt tunnel along a wandering stream. He caught a mink, but something had been improperly done or had gone wrong for the creature had loosened the trap from its stake and fled. Pete followed by going first upstream then downstream, stooping to sniff at air holes from time to time. Naturally, a trap on its foot did nothing to sweeten the mink's customary short temper, and he indicated his displeasure with the free use of his scent glands. Guided by the reek as it seeped through air holes and crevices, Pete finally found the angry animal tangled in a maze of spruce roots more than two miles from where it had pulled loose.

Pete never gave up on any trapped animal until convinced beyond a doubt that he couldn't possibly find it, and in two years he hadn't lost one pelt. Naturally, he knew when to pull his traps. Any man who couldn't read sign well enough to make a very accurate estimate of the fur population had no business trapping. Any trapper who did not leave adequate breeding stock was a fool who deserved no sympathy when his next season's catch wouldn't even pay for the following year's grubstake.

For the present, there was no reason to worry about any unvisited trap. In open water, it was simple to make drowning sets, so that anything caught would still be there when the next rounds were made. Far more important was making those rounds before the freeze-up. Chopping traps out of ice was not the pleasantest job in the world. Land sets were unlikely to need attention. Few land-bound animals moved freely during a storm or while awaiting one. Today, most of them had already repaired to favorite haunts to wait this one out. Pete had taken four prime mink and a nice otter on this trip, but not a single fox, lynx, marten, or anything else that doesn't normally spend much of its time in or near the water.

He was still a half-mile from his down-river camp, dubbed Bull Trout Cabin for the wonderful trout fishing found there, when the snow started. As the scow glided in to the landing, the dogs stood up and made ready to leap ashore the second the craft grounded, so they might be about their everlasting rabbit hunting.

Pete halted them with a stern "No!"

The three turned as one and regarded him with blank astonishment. They were neither packing nor pulling, and it was an unwritten law of the trail that dogs were free to hunt from any overnight camp. Although he was amused by their discomfiture, Pete's second order left no grounds for question.

"Down!" he said sharply.

He grounded the scow, stepped past the sulking dogs, stooped to catch up their chains, and snapped one to the collar of each dog. Leading the three ashore, he tied them to their separate kennels and turned back to the scow. He'd known when he left the Zluskis' that he was gambling on the weather and that he'd probably lose. Now that it was no longer a gamble, he must act accordingly.

With a passing glance for the dogs, who had philosophically decided to make the best of things and were already asleep in their houses, he took his catch to the cabin and prepared to pelt it. The operation involved some complications, since snow blew in if he propped the door open and it was too dark to work if he didn't. After a while, Pete lighted a candle, built a fire, and let the door of his oil-drum stove hang open. He draped his parka on a wooden peg and set to work by the combined light of the candle and the fire.

Proper pelting was as much an art as trapping, but it was one to which some trappers, curiously enough, attached little importance. They had yet to learn that a prime pelt properly handled is more valuable than the same fur wrongly processed. The knife must be used with a deft touch that leaves no clinging flesh or muscle and at the same time makes no cuts in the pelt. The tail bone should be removed rather than merely cut off. The scent glands of certain fur-bearing animals are valuable as a base in preparing lures to attract others. Finally, the pelt must be perfectly stretched.

It was no job that could be done both properly and hastily, so Pete made not the slightest attempt to hurry. But when the stretched pelts finally hung from pegs in the ceiling, to be picked up and taken to the Zluskis' the first time he came back here with a sled, haste became the first order.

Pete thought wistfully of fresh trout, decided that there wasn't time to catch one, and broiled a moose steak which he took from his pack. He cut it with his belt knife, gulped it directly from the broiling rack, to avoid soiling dishes, then made sure the stove was in order, and blew out his candle. He went back into the storm, closing the door of Bull Trout Cabin behind him.

The three dogs looked puzzled when he harnessed them to the towline. He shortened the line as much as possible. Somebody had to steer the scow, and the dogs might decide they didn't have to pull it unless he was able to reach them with the tip of his whip. Pete seated himself in the boat and put his hand on the tiller.

"Hup!" he ordered.

The dogs, purposely left hungry, since they'd work better on empty bellies, blinked in the swirling snow and strained halfheartedly into their harnesses. Pete's lash cracked over their heads.

"Hup!" he repeated.

The lash gave authority to the order. With Baldy setting the pace, all three dogs abandoned pretense in favor of work. Pete raised the hood of his parka against the falling snow. He was doing a fool thing, maybe, to go back up river the same day he'd come down it, but, if so, he'd be a fool.

It made no real difference whether the scow was wintered on blocks at the Zluski house or Pete's Bull Trout Cabin. When the Wisbayah froze, nobody could use it, anyhow. Nor would the scow be any harder to handle after the breakup. If the snow went with the ice, it might be easier. But taking the craft anywhere was out of the question while the river remained frozen. Pete knew only that he would get it back to its rightful owner while he could, if that meant swimming with the towline in his teeth.

He still did not understand what had possessed him that night he came down river and found Hailey at the landing. Nor, although he always thought of her, was it true that he had thought of kissing her! That notion had occurred suddenly. After he had thought of it, he just couldn't help doing it—and while Hailey was in his arms he had wondered why he hadn't thought of it long before. But the instant he released her, he was inundated by a flood of self-reproach and confusion. He had no intention of marrying Hailey—or anyone else—at least, not for a long, long time. He wanted to be foot loose. Then how did this tie up with his making passes at her while he was a guest of the Zluskis?

The impulsive incident might have ended where it began—except for Hailey's ultimatum. What was her interest in that furious, rampaging bull, anyhow? If she had none—and why should she—what was her ulterior motive? Did she think, just because he was a man, practically, that she could lead him around the way she led that big ram of theirs? He'd show her how easily he could be the leader. He'd kill that bull now, surely, if only to prove to her that he could!

Obviously, Hailey had said nothing to her father. If she had complained about his boldness, Casimir would have demanded a explanation long before this. Nevertheless, since that surprising evening, the chasm between Hailey and Pete had grown too wide and deep for either to cross it. Their relations were more frigid than the north wind at its coldest. Even though Casimir appeared not to notice anything unusual, on various occasions when otherwise he would have been alone with Hailey, Pete had deliberately left the house and found some chore to do outside.

This whole troubling, puzzling situation was why he could not be contented with just holding up his end of the work. He provided more than his share of the food, relieved Casimir of all woodchopping chores, gave a hand with others, and otherwise acted in such a manner that he was under the smallest possible obligation to the Zluskis. So the scow *must* go upriver tonight. Hailey must be given no grounds to say—or even to think—that Pete was for any reason keeping anything that rightfully belonged to them at one of his out cabins!

The wind kept steady from the west and, obviously, the snow was not going to fall any faster. Not that it wouldn't pile up anyhow, if the storm lasted two or three days, but it hadn't the makings of a blizzard. Pete's anxiety lessened. The dogs had done nothing all day except ride in the scow or walk with him the few times he'd beached it to take to the ridges and thickets. Still, they'd been active since early morning and might give real trouble if the going got too heavy. Even Baldy, who'd work his pads bloody to get out of a comfortless night into a comfortable kennel, was entirely capable of rebelling if pushed too hard at something that seemed pointless—and Baldy obviously saw no sense in this.

With the coming of night, probably because Pete could no longer see snow falling, the storm seemed to moderate. But although the wind still blew from the west, there was no longer even a feeble glimmer from the sun and the weather turned sharply cold. For a while, Pete kept himself comfortable by buttoning his parka. When that no longer sufficed and he began to shiver, he stopped the dogs, went ashore, and took one of the oars from its lock. Using this to keep the scow fended off the bank, he walked behind the dogs and discovered at once that, not only did the exercise warm him up, but his personal proximity wrought a marked improvement in the speed of the trio.

He'd thought that their progress was unnecessarily slow, but had attributed this partly to the fact that his dogs were working at night during a storm and partly to his own impatience. His sole purpose was to take the scow upriver, with no chance that anything even slightly interesting would spice a monotonous journey. Now he found that the team hadn't merely seemed to travel slowly. Since Megap invariably shirked unless forced to do his share, Pete suspected that Baldy and Jake had been towing the scow and their teammate, too. With his foot only a few inches from Megap's rear, the lagging dog found a new and enthusiastic interest in his duties.

Four times Pete stopped for brief rests. . . . The luminous dial of his wrist watch indicated three o'clock in the morning when he finally heard Folly bark. He reached down to grasp the side of the scow and give a hand as his team pulled the boat out of the water onto new snow. Stooping in the darkness, he unharnessed his dogs and let them slip away. He took his gear from the scow, upended it on blocks, and got three salted fish from the shed. Finding the dogs in their kennels, where he had expected they would be, he gave each a fish and slipped quietly to his own bedroom.

Three and a half hours later he was awakened by the little noises of Casimir building the morning fire, and got up at once. Familiar with routine at the Zluskis', he knew Hailey stayed in bed until the kitchen was comfortable. If he lost no time, perhaps he could be away without facing her at all. At any rate, the sooner he started the better.

Astonished, Casimir whirled to confront him as he entered the room a short time later. "Pete! I thought you'd be down river!"

"I came up last night," the young trapper explained. "The freeze-up won't be far behind this snow and I wanted to bring the scow back while I could."

"That was hardly necessary," his host said mildly. "You could have wintered it through at your Bull Trout Cabin."

"I plan on stringing beaver and muskrat traps from here,"

Pete evaded, "and if the snow doesn't go with the ice, I'd have to wait for a trail. I didn't want to risk losing time."

A question lingered in Casimir's eyes. But rather than voice any doubts concerning such a feeble reason for coming upriver under such conditions, he merely commented, "It must have been rather rough travel last night."

"Not too bad," Pete told him. "The snow's steady but not heavy. Have you been out this morning?"

"Just to the wood box, but I'd guess there's eight to ten inches on the ground and it's still snowing."

Pete nodded absently and fitted this information to his personal plans. Ten inches of new snow presented no insurmountable or even formidable problem, but now was the time to make ready for a possible ten feet before spring. It meant wearing snowshoes, even though he could travel easier and faster without them. He could break a foot of snow, but snowshoes snagged on every hidden log and covered snag, and even experienced travelers could expect unscheduled spills. But wearing snowshoes meant also that he would pack a hard bottom on his trail. By following the same one every trip, and packing each fresh snow, he'd build a hard trail that could be run without snowshoes—if no storm was in prospect. Such a trail would hold up even when some midwinter chinook brought a foretaste of spring to the winter-locked woods and turned everything else to slush. Pete filled the coffeepot and shoved the griddle over a hot lid.

"Don't tell me you're heading right back out?" Casimir queried.

Pete grinned. "I'd better. It's pretty hard to take fur sitting next to a warm stove."

"There's no disputing your logic," Casimir agreed, "but

there's no need to get your own breakfast. Hela does it better. I'll call her."

"Let her sleep." Pete turned to the stove so that Casimir could not see and read his eyes. "I'll rustle for myself."

"But—" Casimir started, then stopped, the question that had been in his eyes now in his tone. Whatever he had intended to say, he did not say it. Instead, he seated himself near the stove and fell into moody silence. His thoughts seemed to wander.

Pete stole a covert glance at him, and a little storm of anxiety raged in his mind. Since coming to live with the Zluskis, he had discovered much that previously he hadn't even suspected. Casimir looked as he'd always looked, but so does a great tree whose insides are rotting away. Casimir would gentle no more wild colts with the strength of his hands. He hadn't even gone back to Raven Pond to salvage what he might from the massacred sheep, nor had he set any traps—and this despite his need of money.

Just how serious was his condition? What would happen to Hailey if Casimir could no longer carry on? She couldn't possibly continue here without help, and there were no relatives to whom she might turn. Without Casimir she'd be lost and—

Pete filled his plate and sat down to eat. He was not his brother's keeper—or his sister's, either—and he'd more than repaid the Zluskis for any favors extended. Let Hailey look to herself. Right now she was deliberately staying out of the kitchen, pretending to be asleep, because she'd heard him talking and didn't want to see him any more than he cared to meet her. Pete finished his breakfast and rose.

Casimir snapped out of the lethargy that had gripped him. "Are you going now?" he asked gravely.

Pete answered, "I think I'd better."

"Hela will be sorry she missed you."

"Tell her I was here," said Pete . . . and left the house.

He was glad to be away, for, suddenly, he was impelled by the same urge that, until now, had overcome him only during the summer or when he dallied too long in Spruce Crossing. He couldn't breathe properly until he was outside. Once there, he cast off this sense of being fettered.

Accompanied by his three heavily-burdened dogs and carrying on his own shoulders any of the food and other essential articles that could not be trusted to a dog's pack, Pete strode across the clearing and into the forest. He'd go back down river, packing his trail through thickets and along ridges which, as yet, he had visited only by grounding the scow and coming up from the Wisbayah. Certainly it would be necessary to dig all his traps out from under the snow and reset them and probably he'd find some new sets. He was in for a long day, but if he kept moving, he'd make it through to Bull Trout Cabin in good time.

He was an estimated third of the way to Bull Trout Cabin when Baldy pricked up his ears and stared. Jake and Megap halted when their master stopped to determine what had attracted Baldy's attention.

Shortly, he saw a moose, coming from an open pond where it had gone to drink, and he knew at first glance that, at last, the enemy was delivered to his judgment. He raised his rifle and sighted. Snow was falling, but not heavily, and the bull was walking very slowly. Pete's finger tightened on the trigger.

A split second before he exerted that final bit of pressure which would have exploded the cartridge and brought the great bull down in bloody snow, Pete lowered his rifle. He stood motionless as the bull faded from sight. It was not the time, he assured himself. The moose had shed both antlers. Let him grow new ones, so that he might be humbled at the very peak of pride and strength. Revenge would then be twice as sweet. But, as he resumed his journey down the ridges, Pete heard very clearly a voice he had heard before.

"Don't you ever kill that big bull! Not any time or for any reason! If you do, I don't want you ever to come near me again!"

7

GOOD-BY TO PETE

ALTHOUGH she knew very well that both her father and Peter were outside, Hailey Zluski gave a quick glance all about the kitchen when she entered it, as though someone might see her and there was reason why he should not, before she tiptoed to the window. She stood to one side, where she could look without being looked at. For a wistful moment, she yearned for the limitless powers that were granted her when she roamed the private world of her own fancy. Magic alone could prevail here, for nothing else could turn the calendar backward. Everything would become right, if only it were possible to return from this early springtime to September and start all over again.

If that were the case, Pete would have known exactly when to expect the great bull's charge. Since he'd have been prepared, of course he would not have let the dogs push him into the pool. So who would have blamed him, or any man, for standing his ground and killing a beast when his single alternative was to let the beast kill him? If it had happened that way, the incident would have furnished food for many discussions and everyone would have known a heartfelt gratitude because Pete had lived to tell of it.

Also, she and her father, for their part, never would have left their sheep at Raven Pond with Folly their only protector. They'd have stayed with the flock, brought it safely home, and been happy to find Pete waiting. Having the flock, of course, would not restore her father's failing health. But there would be no need to worry over both a bad physical condition and a worse mental ailment that was robbing him of hope. He knew that he hadn't even a faint chance of starting over again.

The autumn and winter that had just dragged by would have been a joyous time, with special treats and games whenever Pete came home and all three warmly delighted with his remarkable success on the trap lines. They—

Hailey's aching heart showed in her sorrowful eyes as the sight of her father's horses, wearing packsaddles and tethered to a picket line, wrenched her from the happy world she would like to have to the tragic one she had. . . . There was no going back and no undoing what was done.

Tagged by Pete's dogs, all three in a mood of tail-wagging amiability, since it was apparent that horses were going to do the work, Pete and her father came in view. Each carried a bale of fur. They dropped their burdens beside Aunt Anna, the most patient of the Zluskis' horses, and made ready to pack her first. Bucephalus, snorting overlord of their little herd and the most inclined to resent burdens, would be the last packed because he needed watching. It was much less than a joy to have a pack bucked all over a half-acre lot a split second before applying the final hitch! Even after the diamond hitch was thrown and Bucephalus could no longer buck his load, he was not above trying to roll on it.

The first two bales were lifted into place, Aunt Anna never moving as they were secured. They seemed an awkward load and much too heavy for one horse, but they were not. Cured furs occupied space out of all proportion to their weight, and doubtless Aunt Anna's pack—as well as that of the other horses and perhaps the dogs, too—would increase to as much as may be tied on a packsaddle. Pete had made a fabulous catch during the past winter, the kind that haunts every trapper's dreams but seldom graces his fur shed. Hailey tried to remember its value, as estimated by the young trapper, and recalled only vaguely that it amounted to many thousands of dollars.

The total impressed Casimir as much as it pleased Pete—but, suddenly, Hailey saw it as a trifling thing. She and her father had never had so much money and there was no reason to suppose they ever would have. But if the laborer was truly worthy of his hire, Pete's reward was small enough in comparison with the labor he'd expended.

He had shown himself no mercy. On the trail from dawn to dark, he needed half the night to process his catch. He had denied himself a Christmas holiday in Spruce Crossing—a midwinter break so precious to most trappers that a hundred or more miles of snow-locked trail was no obstacle to those who wished to enjoy it. He had even defied the weather. Only once, during the winter's worst blizzard, with visibility never exceeding two feet, had he stayed off his trails and then he had chafed until the storm lulled. When the spring breakup brought open water, and ideal beaver and muskrat trapping, he was off again. Working for as many hours as he could see, he postponed taking his catch to Spruce Crossing until even the packed trails rotted under the warming sun and he couldn't go until the snow melted. . . . But he was going now.

Hailey whirled away from the window and, as she did so, a little spark of hope glowed within her. It shed a very faint warmth that cooled immediately. Magic powers were a feeble help indeed, for refusing to look any longer made not the slightest difference. Although she could not see them, she knew that her father and Pete were still packing the horses. When they finished, Pete would take them down the trail.

It was a very bitter prospect, and somehow, it was so cruelly undeserved. Wounds alone were not a proper legacy of friendship. Hailey thought of the Pete she had once known, the grinning big brother who was flattered if she teased him and who was honestly worried because he considered her too fragile for the life she was leading. He had been a dear intimate whom she knew as well as she knew her father—and understood much better, because he was less complex than her deeply experienced parent. She had known him so intimately that she could even read his thoughts.

But she reluctantly admitted that the Pete in her own thoughts was not the one who was now packing their horses.

It was very bewildering. This Pete was a stranger—or nearly so—and how had the change been brought about? Hailey thought again of the great bull, doing her best to place him in a proper perspective. As a brute, he was no more significant than any other of his kind. But as a symbol, he represented roots so deep and ideals so lofty that life without them would mean nothing to her. Pete's desire for revenge was both human and understandable, but his inability to rise above such a mean motive could never be condoned. That was all she had tried to tell him the day she found the bull and met Pete at the scow landing. Oh, how could she have told him so clumsily or so haughtily?

Presently—there was some magic left—her memory took her back to that meeting. She told herself that she had responded to Pete when he had embraced and kissed her because she had been petrified by astonishment, but she couldn't help sharing this assurance with a notion that she had not wanted to resist. Occasionally, before that, she had beguiled herself by wondering vaguely and romantically how it would feel if Pete kissed her, but such a possibility had seemed so improbable that, deep down, she had decided she'd never know. Now that she did, she knew also that it would be far easier to see Pete go if she must still wonder.

Hailey stifled a powerful desire to steal again to the window. Even if there were some way to reconcile Pete's outlook with her own conception of right and wrong, there would still be barriers. Although she was of the New World, her whole background and training were rooted in the Old, where girls were the objects of courtship rather than the instigators. She would not know how to forsake the precepts that had come to her through her father, and to him in turn through a thousand years of history, during which all known rules for living were tested so that those proven both decent and good might be retained and applied.

Suddenly, Hailey thought of the refuge she desperately needed and fled to her own nook in the living room. Her books were there on floor-to-ceiling shelves, but they were no longer friendly as she had left them. They had become almost alien, so withdrawn that once warm and meaningful titles were no more than cold and meaningless words now. Her burden of despair was doubled by a crushing sense of futility. She and her father had never regarded books as other than a foremost necessity. Were they? Or were they just a ridiculously defiant declaration that the Zluskis' environment might be primitive but their erudition remained? What did culture mean to a charging bull moose? Or, for that matter, what did it mean to a trapper?

Then, with jolting suddenness, Hailey's crumbling world stopped falling apart. From the ashes of destroyed hope there came new strength. She understood, wonderingly, that it had not and never could be imparted by her books, or anything tangible, but that her sheer misery of heart and mind had taught her how to tap a hidden well within herself. With it came a curious sensation that a blindfold she'd always worn, but not even suspected until it was there no more, had been lifted from her eyes. Never before had she attained such a lucid understanding. At last, she knew exactly how her father had felt on that terrible night when his own world collapsed. Finally, she understood clearly that he could not possibly have done anything except try to put the remaining pieces back together.

The thousand years of history that had produced his ideals were also a thousand years of tyranny and oppression. The human spirit had proven superior to the brute, and, in that moment of clear insight, Hailey knew it would always triumph. She and her father were stronger than any ills that might assail them. Whatever they might be called upon to face, overpowering fear would never be a part of it.

Hailey was as serene as the cloudless May sky outside when her father came into the kitchen. For the first time since she'd known he was ill, Hailey faced her father with no anxiety that her concerned heart might be revealed to him in her eyes.

Casimir had his daughter's warm sympathy, but he never would be degraded by her pity. He deserved better than that.

"Pete's ready to go," Casimir said. "He'd come in to say good-by, except he's afraid Bucephalus might act up. Will you come out?"

"Of course," Hailey answered quietly.

She slipped her arm through his and walked beside him to say her farewells. A limber stick in one hand, Bucephalus' lead rope in the other, and watching the recalcitrant animal warily, Pete swung to face them, while still managing to keep a wary eye on the unruly horse. He shuffled like an awkward boy and Hailey's heart went out to him. The days that loomed ahead promised to be empty days indeed, but at last she had become complete mistress of herself. She masked her face with a bright smile and hid her feelings with happy wishes for him.

"Good luck, Pete! I hope you find a rising fur market and get three times what you expect."

"Yeah. Yeah." Pete looked at the ground and Hailey knew that, if both hands had not already been filled he would have thrust them in his pockets. "Yes– It–it was wonderful of you two to take me in."

Casimir Zluski said with courtly grace, "It was our delight and privilege."

"Of course, Pete," Hailey agreed. "We– Watch out!"

Bucephalus lunged sideways and Pete fought him to a standstill. The incident restored some measure of his composure. Horses he understood. He turned back to the Zluskis.

"Ten miles of trail will take the ginger out of him and he'll be easy to handle tomorrow," he said. "I'd better picket him tonight, though, or he may take it into his head to come home. The rest won't leave if he can't."

"A sensible precaution," Casimir murmured.

"Well– Wel–" Again Pete threatened to become lost. Then, "Thanks–thanks for everything!" he blurted out. "I'll send the horses back from Spruce Crossing."

"Good luck!" Hailey cried.

Her father added, "Godspeed, Pete."

Leading Bucephalus and driving the rest of the horses with the unburdened dogs ranging from one side to the other, then hurrying to catch up, Pete crossed the clearing and turned to wave just before he entered the forest. Father and daughter waved back . . . and Pete was gone.

Casimir Zluski, a little hesitant, turned to Hailey.

"He said he'll send the horses back."

"He will," Hailey assured him.

"But–" Casimir was groping. "Do you not understand? He isn't coming back."

Hailey shrugged lightly. "He said nothing about it to me."

"Not even for his gear!" Casimir exclaimed.

"He has a stake," Hailey reminded her father. "When he sells his fur, he'll be able to go where he pleases and buy what he needs. At last, Pete has all he ever wanted."

Casimir asked, "And what is that?"

"If I may fall back on local vernacular, he wants to be foot-loose," Hailey replied.

Casimir said gravely, "No. I think not."

Mildly surprised, Hailey turned to her father. "What is your analysis of Mr. Gant's ultimate goal?"

"That of all thinking men," Casimir told her. "He wants a wife, a home, children to give to the world who, if fortune smiles, will do some of the many tasks that must be done and which he cannot do. Only thus may he hope to leave the world a little better than he found it—and who does not live for that end lives in vain."

"Dad!" Hailey made no attempt to conceal her astonishment.

"It is true, Hela," her father said quietly. "Pete has little formal education, but he does not lack intelligence and he leans toward goodness. In time he will be good. I have watched—"

Casimir stopped speaking. "Go on," Hailey prompted.

"Perhaps I should not have mentioned this," Casimir said with a trace of embarrassment, "but I have watched him many times and he is not practiced in subtle matters, such as hiding what he truly feels. Pete is in love with you, Hela."

"No!" Hailey gasped.

"Yes," her father corrected her. "If we see him no more on the Wisbayah, we must not believe he has surrendered to wanderlust. Wander he may, but he will do so in the hope that new faces, new scenes, and new experiences will so fill his mind that there will be no room for the torment of hopeless love."

"You've been reading confession magazines!" Hailey accused him.

"No," Casimir dissented, "I've been reading a man's thoughts as they were written on a man's face."

Hailey laughed lightly—and at the same time breathed a prayer of thanks for newfound inner strength. All in a moment, she had ceased being partly a child and had become entirely a woman.

"This horrible suspense!" she teased. "Tell me the ending!"

Her father remained grave. "That is known only to the God

who created Pete Gant, for He alone knows the ingredients in this particular creation."

"Please translate," Hailey urged. "Epigrams are so confusing."

"Leander swam the Hellespont for his love," said Casimir. "Abelard flouted death—and disgrace, too—for Heloise. Because his love inspired immortal poetry, it created immortality for Robert Browning. Shah Jehan expressed in the Taj Mahal his deep devotion to the mourned Mumtaz Mahal. There are numerous others like them—but so are there many who gave way to bitterness and accepted defeat. Whether Pete returns depends wholly on his heart. It will either accept rejection or send him back to fight again for what he holds most dear."

"Oh!" Hailey ejaculated. "Now I envy Mother!"

"Why do you say that?" her father asked.

"Because she married you," she answered, and slipped a hand into his. "Forward the Zluskis! The fighting Zluskis!"

She escorted him into the house . . . then flew to the kitchen window the instant he entered his study. Of course her father was mistaken, but the mere fact that he thought Pete loved her set her heart beating like a frightened bird's. She looked out of the window, down the trail . . . and did not turn away at once when she saw the clearing and forest only. She let herself dream that her father was right. Perhaps Pete had already turned back, and, in a moment or two, she would see him as he came forward to fight again for that which he held most dear.

He did not come and, after a while, Hailey turned away from the window. She was vaguely grateful because the pain was no more, but unaware that she felt nothing at all except a numbing dullness. Never again could she walk in her private world. It had been stricken out of existence—and all the magic with it.

But the strength did not desert her. As she turned her back on Pete Gant, Hailey did not forget to remind herself that it was still, "Forward the fighting Zluskis!"

8

PETE'S FLING

RIDING his own horse and driving Casimir Zluski's little band, Tom Malone rode out of Spruce Crossing and disappeared, heading westward. . . . Pete turned away, and his three dogs rose to follow. Tom Malone was always a good man for any job, but he'd never take any except when he had a lean year on the trap lines. Pete was lucky to have been able to get him to return Casimir's horses.

The borrowed horses no longer his obligation, Pete continued on down the street. A man whose face he knew, but whose name he did not, hailed him.

"Doggone! I figured you'd have your own private car and a man to drive it by this time!"

"I'm going to arrange that now."

Pete grinned amiably. With thirteen thousand dollars' worth of furs—as far as anyone knew the best season's catch ever brought into Spruce Crossing—his fame had spread as quickly as wildfire gossip could spread it. A great many people he neither knew nor cared about suddenly knew him. He waved at another well-wisher, then ducked between two buildings into an alley and made his way to an outlandish house and yard. He had acquired a bit of swagger in his walk.

Built of logs, roofed with discarded tin signs that proclaimed the virtues of various articles popular in Spruce Crossing for thirty years back, and decorated with rows of beer bottle caps, the house belonged to a trapper grown too old for the trails. The yard was fenced, but in a highly unorthodox manner, with such diverse materials as discarded bed springs, wagon wheels, strips of poultry netting, and peeled saplings set upright in the ground. Six empty dog kennels were spaced far enough apart to prevent fighting when they were occupied.

Pete halted at the gate and yelled, "Hi, Tunk!"

"Hi yourself an' beat it," came the snarled answer.

Pete laughed. "Come on out, Tunk. We won't bite."

"Whyn't ya say it was you?" Tunk Abbot growled.

He came from the house, a huge old man who had once strung his traps along creeks since converted to the Spruce Crossing water system. He had broiled his moose steaks where the hotel stood. A proud old man, he eked out a living boarding dogs for town-bound trappers and Pete wouldn't think of leaving his elsewhere. You had to know work dogs before you could give them proper care.

Pete called, "All three, I don't know how long."

Tunk Abbot came and leaned on the gate. He looked at the bills Pete handed him but withheld comment. Tunk charged a dollar a day per dog, payable in advance, if the owner had it, and some other time if he didn't. Pete had just given him six months' advance, but more than once Tunk had boarded Pete's dogs and waited for his pay until the young trapper had rebuilt his shattered finances. The next time, Pete probably would have a balance due, so that credit system satisfied all concerned.

"Heard you made a haul," Tunk stated. "Heard you fetched in thirty-one thousand dollars' worth o' fuf."

Pete said, "The wind gathered a lot of leaves as it blew. I brought just over thirteen thousand."

"What's wrong with that?" the old man demanded.

"Nothing. I'm satisfied."

"You should be. I froze my feet for twice's many winters as you've had birthdays, and the best take I ever got came to just under seven thousand."

"Fur was cheaper then."

"So was fun," Tunk asserted, "as you're due to find out."

Pete said, "Come to think of it, it's past due I found out."

"Since it wouldn't do a lick of good anyhow, I won't tell you to cache something away in the bank while you have it," Tunk said. "If you had sense enough to do that, you'd have too much to be a trapper. Come get your dogs when you're broke."

"That'll be awhile. Good-by, you three. Behave yourselves."

Tunk snorted derisively. Pete spun on his heel and walked away. His dogs, his final obligation, had just been turned over to Tunk Abbot. With plenty of money in his wallet, plenty of reserves in the bank—in spite of Tunk Abbot's doubts—and accountable to nobody for its spending, he was free as any man can be. He went back onto Snowshoe Street and turned toward Hackey's Moosehead Pavilion.

The westbound train slowed for the station and stopped, panting impatiently, as though irritated over interrupting its journey for a place so insignificant. Two sports fishermen got off and two trappers, Ole and Hjalmar Toenesson, who made a summer business of guiding sports-minded anglers, met them. It was a good business that paid well—in some seasons a lot better than trapping—but it was for those who wanted it. A guide became his client's man, therefore he couldn't be his own, Pete thought.

Hjalmar turned, saw Pete, and hailed him. "Pete! Wait a minute, will you?"

Pete stopped to wait for the giant Norseman. Hjalmar came near and nodded toward Ole and their guests.

He said, "These two fellas, Pete, they want to go back in an' me an' Ole ain't but thirty or so miles out of town. You mind if we take 'em to fish out of your cabin at Two Moose?"

"I don't mind if they move in permanently," Pete said.

Hjalmar's face clouded. "Ain't you goin' back?"

Pete said decisively, "Nope."

"Sorry to hear it," Hjalmar said. "Still, what with the stake you got an' no family to tie you down, I guess you do feel like movin' on. I wonder somethin', Pete."

"Yes?"

"Ole an' me's been thinkin' about a new trap line for some time. If it ain't pushin' things an' you really made up your mind to leave, would you sell out to us?"

"Sure," Pete agreed quickly.

"You figured out a price?"

Pete answered, "Until you asked me, I hadn't given it a thought. Why not look things over while you're there and see if it's what you want? If it is, we can get together through the mails."

"Suits us, if it does you."

"It suits me," Pete declared. "Good fishing."

Hjalmar said, "If we don't find it at Two Moose, we ain't goin' to find it. Come say hello to Ole an' the dudes."

"No, thanks," Pete declined. "I'm already late for an appointment with Hackey."

"Oh!" Hjalmar grinned understandingly. "Stay out of jail."

"I'll try," Pete promised.

He left the sunny street for the cool and dim interior of Hackey's Pavilion. It was the usual small-town pleasure palace, all of which seem founded on the same set of plans, and the personal touches that supposedly make them different serve somehow only to make them seem more alike. There was a mahogany bar with the usual mirror and rows of polished glasses and assorted beverages. The bar was flanked on either wall by a stuffed moose head—in other localities they might have been antelope, elk, or buck deer—whose glassy eyes were eternally focused on the same spot. There were bar stools, tables and chairs, booths, and the omniscient juke box. The town had never been given reason to complain about Hackey's place.

Hackey, the only man in Spruce Crossing who never wore anything except a neat suit, complete with white shirt and tie, and whose facial shrubbery was confined to a hair-line mustache, bent over backward for the dual purpose of maintaining his standing in the community and being ready to pick up all opportunities that came within reach.

A couple of transients seated in a booth were so fascinated by whatever they were discussing that they seemed to have forgotten the beer at their elbows. Albion Dalhart, a once-prosperous merchant who'd started sliding and found himself unable to stop, stood at the bar, nursing a drink and talking with lame Greg Harkness, the bartender. A rather attractive girl Pete did not know, but for whom he had only one casual glance, sat alone at a table. Hackey—if he had another name nobody knew it—had not yet appeared. Pete walked to the bar and Greg Harkness turned to him.

"First one's on the house, Pete. What'll it be?"

Pete said, with a hint of smugness in his voice, "Hackey wouldn't approve of this on the house. Set me up one on my own, Greg."

Albion Dalhart spoke in a curiously subdued and almost servile tone, as though he had forfeited the respect of others when he lost his own. "I heard you brought in a nice catch, Pete."

"Nice enough to pay all my back bills, Albion." Pete handed the other a twenty-dollar bill. "I didn't have this the first time I came through here and stopped at your store, but you had what I needed. Thanks a lot."

"But—"

Albion Dalhart started and stopped. He couldn't remember Pete's first appearance in Spruce Crossing. At various times he had sold the young trapper something or other—but seldom on credit. He pocketed the bill, and the look he bestowed on Pete was pathetic in its gratitude—but it was not the money in itself that had caused this. When he lost his pride, he discovered that he was capable of begging. Now, for the first time in years, he knew all over again how it felt to be treated as something besides a beggar.

Pete took up the glass with the drink Greg had poured and gulped half of it down. He sputtered and choked and put one hand on the bar to steady himself. He hadn't thought he would react like this to his first drink!

Albion Dalhart called out, "You'd better take it easy, Pete."

"Mind your own business!" Pete's manner became a little truculent as he reached for his glass once more.

"Come along with me, Pete."

Pete blinked a hole in the red cloud that floated before his eyes and saw Albion Dalhart beside him.

"Sure," he agreed. "Where we goin'?"

"You're coming home with me." The man put a firm arm around Pete's shoulders. As the two started for the door, they passed Hackey, who was leading the strange girl toward the bar. Hackey put out a detaining hand but Albion Dalhart brushed it aside and continued the march for the door.

Two hours later, Pete woke up to find himself lying on a couch in the room in back of Albion Dalhart's rundown store. After a cup of black coffee and a long, serious talk with the shopkeeper, he headed for the railroad station.

Three days later, the soft spring evening was melting into a warm spring night when Pete ascended the front steps of a pleasant suburban home and hesitantly touched the bell.

"My name is Pete Gant," he said to the middle-aged man who came to the door, and who did not look like Casimir Zluski but still reminded him of Casimir. "I was at the University and they told me Professor George MacClain is the man I want."

"I'm George MacClain. What can I do for you, Mr. Gant?"

Pete answered gravely, "I need someone who can teach me about books. I know how to read, but not always what I'm reading. I want to find out."

"And you want me to teach you?"

"If you will," Pete said. "The hours will be long and the work hard, I know, but—but the pay will be in proportion, I can promise you. Will you help me?" The pleading voice sounded very earnest—and very youthful.

George MacClain held the door wide open. "Won't you please come in, Mr. Gant?" he invited, with an understanding smile.

9

A SPATE OF VISITORS

LAMBING TIME brought to light an unexpected and cruelly disheartening aftermath of the wolf pack's raid to the Zluskis. The thirty-three breeding ewes that remained produced a total of only twenty-three lambs, and the tenderest care and most skilled nursing at Hailey's command were not enough to save three of those. A fourth squeaked through by the narrowest of margins, but, after a week of illness and three days' convalescence, it acquired an unshakable conviction that Hailey was its true mother. It dogged her steps wherever she went, and the ewe was no more interested in accepting her offspring than the lamb was inclined to desert Hailey.

Whimsically named Whiffenpoof by Casimir Zluski, for it had indeed gone sadly astray, it was already a complete nuisance. But there was nothing for it except to be patient and hope to find some way of returning the lamb to the flock. The thirteenth attempt to effect a reconciliation between the ewe and her baby proving as fruitless as the first twelve, Hailey sighed and turned from the flock to the house. She looked speculatively at Whiffenpoof, frolicking beside her, and stooped to pat her head. Casimir had wryly suggested that one certain way to end the problem lay in converting Whiffenpoof to lamb chops. Hailey would have indignantly rejected such a notion, even if snatching the sickly creature from the jaws of death had not made her doubly precious. With a spring increase of only twenty, it was obvious that the fighting Zluskis must start battling for the future of their flock. Not a single sheep was expendable.

Hailey sighed, reminded herself to count her blessings, and found a measure of solace in the thought that their home clearing provided ample summer-long forage for the sadly depleted flock. Since it was unnecessary to seek distant pastures, it was automatically needless to run the risks involved. Folly had become such a zealous guardian that he wouldn't leave his charges even to eat, but insisted on having all meals brought to

him. His roared challenge greeted every alien thing that entered the clearing, and Casimir and Hailey both kept rifles ready for action. They had lost most of their sheep, but at least they could defend what remained.

Before entering the house, Hailey stopped to watch the setting sun reflected from the river. A river of purest gold, she thought, and anyone's for the taking. Why seek hidden wealth, and hidden risks, when this was far more beautiful? Then she grinned, thought wistfully of what might be done with even a modest amount of tangible wealth, and ran into the house.

Whiffenpoof, who thought having a human mother made her human and therefore entitled to her own place in the family circle, stood at the screen door and voiced disapproval in a series of trembling baas when Hailey shut her out. Casimir swept frowning from his study.

He snapped, "Since we seem to have exhausted all sane

possibilities for quieting that hideous racket, suppose we muzzle the creature, Hela?"

"She'll be hungry and tired, too, in a very short time and go nibble grass," Hailey soothed.

Casimir said caustically, "The hunger I concede. You yourself have daily milked the unfortunate ewe, and she most surely consorted with some horned demon, since neither Vladimir nor any of my lesser rams ever sired this monster. She has had all her mother's milk, but even such a generous supply is too little, for, in addition, she crops enough grass to fatten any five adult sheep or nourish any ten. The weariness I not only dispute, but I declare that she isn't even capable of such a feeling. Last night she maintained her weird cacophony at this very door for fifty-eight minutes!"

"It was exactly twenty-nine," Hailey bantered. "I timed her by the kitchen clock."

Her father, Hailey thought, remained as perfect an imitation of an approaching thunderstorm as any human will ever achieve. There was a short interval of quiet, the lull just before the storm breaks. Then the sheets of rain came in all their fury.

"She is indeed silent when she's hungry!" Casimir raged. "Unfortunately, when the pangs of hunger are stilled, no matter how fleetingly, she regains her voice. Last night, and do not tell me that it was not past midnight, for I also have a timepiece and have long understood how to read the same, she blatted at the door for no less than an hour and a quarter! When I finally was driven past the point of endurance and came determined to quiet her with the ax, she was sleeping most peacefully in the wood box!

"My wood box!" Casimir roared, as though to emphasize his argument. "The same from which I pluck our wood! Do you know, Hela, that sheep and lambs—especially this lamb—have no standards whatever of personal cleanliness?"

Hailey remained patient and soothing. "Whiffy sleeps in the wood box only because it's the nearest thing she can find to the box I kept her in while she was sick. It isn't her fault because she thinks she's human. She thinks I'm her mother and is convinced—"

"That I'm her father!" The outraged bellow of an aging and ailing Casimir gave Hailey a clear glimpse of what her father might have done when young. "It's degrading, Hela! We must—"

As suddenly as it had started, the storm lulled and then stopped. Casimir's gentle smile was the sun that always came when black clouds departed. All in a moment, he was again the great but, at the same time, humble father Hailey knew and loved, and whose greatness was rooted in his very humility.

He said softly, "In view of the way I've been roaring, perhaps one of the greatest of scriptural prophecies will be realized if I go lie down beside Whiffenpoof. I'm sorry, Hela, and I wonder at myself. A little lamb should be incapable of arousing any man's anger."

Hailey said firmly, "I'm afraid women aren't that noble, Dad. Whiffy gets me on edge, too, and never think she doesn't, but I'm afraid we'll just have to put up with her until we find some way to make her go back to the flock."

Hailey turned to her evening chores, and managed to keep her thoughts to herself. A little lamb was indeed a pitiful object for her father's anger. Only last fall, a pack of freebooting wolves had proved unable to arouse that much, but, of late, he surrendered with increasing readiness to irritation. Nor was it major problems that set him off, but always some petty annoyance that formerly he would not have stooped to notice. It was as much a symptom of illness as was his physical failing, and as such it must be accepted and understood.

Presently, true to Hailey's prediction, the hungry Whiffenpoof stopped trying to push the screen door through and rambled off to nibble grass. A moment afterward, Folly voiced such a blasting roar that the frightened lamb came skittering back to the door. Hailey and her father went to the door and her heart missed a beat.

Tail streaming away from his back, black mane flying, Bucephalus galloped out of the forest and at once fell to cropping the familiar grasses of his beloved home pasture. Four of Casimir's other horses followed, but Hailey could not relax until Aunt Anna, who clearly saw even a homecoming as no good reason to hurry, sauntered down the trail to join her herd mates.

After Aunt Anna came, there was no point in further looking. There was really none when Bucephalus appeared, Hailey thought, for Pete Gant would have ridden the most fiery of all the horses–if he were coming. He was not coming, but he was very true to his promise and had sent the borrowed horses back. The rider who came on the heels of Aunt Anna was Tom Malone.

Hailey said, "I'll set another place," and turned dejectedly back to her cooking.

Casimir left to help Tom with his horse. Hailey conjured up a mental image of the man who had come.

Whipcord thin and youthfully supple, despite graying streaks in his black hair, Tom Malone was noted for an ability to do anything well except talk. In addition to a talent for getting things done, he had a knack for seeing through complex problems that baffled others, and suggesting a solution so absurdly simple and so glaringly obvious that anyone who had been grappling with the same problem was always inclined to wonder how the same answer had escaped him. As sparing of conversation as he was lavish with his abilities.

When Casimir brought their guest in, Hailey's smile gave weight to her, "It's nice to see you again, Tom."

"Thanks, Hailey." Tom returned the smile.

Casimir questioned, "It's four years since you came this way, isn't it?"

"Three."

"Providence directed you," Casimir asserted. "That lamb had both of us on the edge of insanity."

Hailey glanced up. "Did you take care of Whiffenpoof, Tom?"

"Yup."

"And most ingeniously," Casimir stated. "Lacking both maternal and filial ties, Tom resorted to a practical expedient. Whiffenpoof is now bound to her mother with a length of rope."

"The ewe will kill her!" Hailey protested.

"So I thought," said her father, "but, as a positive guarantee of sweet relations, Tom dusted Whiffenpoof with sugar. The ewe is busy licking it off. She seems to want as much of this child as she can get."

"What's Whiffy doing?" Hailey asked.

Casimir answered, "Thanks to Tom, the broken family is broken no longer."

Hailey turned to Tom. "That was clever of you!"

Letting a bashful grin and a self-demeaning shrug speak for

him, Tom managed perfectly to convey his considered opinion that it was nothing, at least nothing anyone could not have done as well, and perhaps better, if he'd just kept his eyes open and thought about what he saw. With the same gestures, he faithfully conformed to those laws of decorum which demand a refutation of all compliments and adroitly sidestepped the painful necessity of so much as a single spoken word.

Hailey served the meal, reproaching herself as she did so for a nagging little thought that refused to be banished. Of all the people who might have returned the horses, why did it have to be Tom Malone? Why not somebody who knew how to talk—preferably about Pete?

"Was Pete looking well?" she asked guardedly.

"Yep."

"What will he do with his dogs?"

"Board 'em."

Casimir asked with genuine interest, "Did he discuss his plans for the future?"

"Nope."

Hailey conjectured, "I doubt if anyone must be told what they'll be for the immediate future. With money burning a hole in his pockets, he'll do as any other trapper would and have himself a grand fling."

Tom grinned fleetingly. "Likely."

"He did rather well, didn't he?" Casimir asked.

"Thirteen thousand."

Hailey gasped. Pete himself had estimated his catch as worth nine thousand, and that much only if the market was good. He had either been unusually conservative or—she could see no harm in believing this—all her good wishes had come true and he'd sold on a boom market. Hailey found herself happy for

Pete. She looked almost enviously at Tom Malone, who had beheld and talked with Pete three full days after she last saw him, and yearned to have the image that had been in Tom's eyes re-created in her own through magic words that could spring only from an understanding heart.

There was such a vast store of things she longed to know, but, even as the thought occurred, it was nullified by another. Tom Malone wouldn't even know how to go about telling her how Pete had looked, and if he was happy, and whether he needed attention. He wouldn't even understand why she was hungry for a thousand-and-one intimate and personal little details which, in his opinion, were Pete's business alone. For all Tom's worth and all his ingenuity, he lacked an understanding heart.

Early the next morning, Hailey watched Tom leave, riding his own horse across the clearing and stopping to wave a final farewell just before he disappeared in the forest. Hailey waved back.

Then she turned to the flock, giving Folly an affectionate pat as he wagged to meet her. Standing near her mother, Whiffenpoof regarded her with cold suspicion as she knelt to untie Tom's rope. With no second glance for Hailey, the well-licked Whiffenpoof butted her mother's flank and took her nourishment directly from the most ancient source of all food.

That night, Hailey was again preparing supper when Folly's warning roar brought her to the door. A string of pack horses she did not recognize trotted tiredly out of the forest into the clearing. Following came four riders, of whom two were definitely strangers and two seemed familiar. Nearing the house, and knowing they'd reached the end of this day's journey, the pack horses stopped and waited expectantly for someone to come take their packs.

As the riders drew near, Hailey recognized Hjalmar and Ole Toenesson. They were trappers who guided during the spring and summer season, she remembered, and Pete usually let them use his Two Moose Cabin. She stepped outside.

"Hello!" she called gaily.

"Hi, Hailey!" Hjalmar boomed. "I seen Pete!"

"You did?" Suddenly Hjalmar, whose outward appearance gave him more than a superficial resemblance to a sleepy Saint Bernard, acquired some of the more appealing points of Adonis in her eyes.

"Yah! We'll take care of our stuff an' come in! These two dudes are John Wentworth an' Art Satterlee! I'll send 'em in!" He turned to the pair, and, as though they might have missed hearing what nothing else for a quarter of a mile in any direction could possibly have missed, roared, "Go on in! That pretty girl at the door is Hailey Zluski! Her pa will be around some place!"

More than a little embarrassed by an introduction that lacked any semblance of formality, and confused by such surroundings where they had expected wilderness only, the pair surrendered their saddle horses to the brothers Toenesson and came forward. They were middle-aged, Hailey saw, and neither could possibly be mistaken for anything except highly placed executives of some responsible business. Certainly they were welcome, and it was a foregone conclusion that they would also be congenial and delightful company. Hailey had yet to know a sports fisherman or hunter who came so far and was not.

When the two men were near enough, she said graciously, "Welcome, gentlemen."

"That is very kind of you, Miss Zluski." Art Satterlee, the darker and stockier of the two, was doing his best to conjure up a rule of courtesy that might apply when one met a girl so gracious and lovely where one expected to meet only moose or grizzlies. "John Wentworth and I really have no intention of barging in on you. With your permission, we'll ask our intrepid guides to set up camp and—"

Hjalmar, overhearing, bawled, "Stop bendin' your jaw an' go in, Art! We set up no camp here!"

"I surely hope not." Casimir Zluski had approached so quietly that no one knew he was present until he spoke over Hailey's shoulder. "Hela, you have met these gentlemen?"

Hailey introduced the pair, and her father, who had the visitors entirely in his spell, escorted them inside. Hailey left them alone. Few guests who knew how to meet Casimir on his own level ever came to the Wisbayah, but the few who did brought their own magic tonic and left her father exhilarated and happy for days. As a rule, Hailey liked to participate in such conversations, but, this time, she was far more interested in the brothers Toenesson and anything they might say about Pete.

Ole and Hjalmar appeared, shaggy as grizzly bears but gentle as Aunt Anna. Blonde giants, their hamlike hands could soothe a frightened horse, tie a delicate fly, or raise a quarter ton of dead weight. Masters of their own element, the out-of-doors, neither had ever acknowledged the slightest reason for even trying to master anything else.

Hjalmar made a playful stab at Hailey's cheek. "By golly! You grow prettier every time I see you! If I didn't already have me a wife an' nine kids, I'd be settin' on Casimir's doorstep seven nights a week!"

"To think what I've missed!" Hailey moaned. "I'd not be the one to sweep you off, either, if you didn't already have a wife and nine children."

"Hear that!" Hjalmar bellowed. "Hear that, Ole! Even Hailey Zluski could like me! Didn't I tell you?"

"Yah," the less boisterous Ole agreed. "But you better not tell Olga."

"Better not at that." Hjalmar grinned. "Hailey wouldn't crack me with a broom, but there's no tellin' about Olga. Pete says he stayed with you an' Casimir the winter through, Hailey?"

"Indeed he did," said Hailey, and wondered why she could not make her voice attain a properly frivolous lilt. "It's the first season he ever worked from any base except Two Moose."

Hjalmar said blandly, "Then Pete's sure enough put in his last season at Two Moose. He sold his line."

"What!" Hailey gasped.

"Yup," Hjalmar asserted, and both brothers remained happily oblivious to the distress in the girl's eyes. "Sold to Ole an' me. Pete ain't set a price, but he says we can do that by mail."

"I see." Hailey hoped she sounded decently casual. "Is Pete going away?"

"That's what he told me."

"Did he say where?" she pursued.

"He don't know that his own self." Hjalmar shrugged. "With all that money, an' no family to hold him down, it could be any place in the world. I don't blame him, an' maybe I'd do the same if I was in Pete's shoes. It must be fun to look at somethin' new now an' again."

"Yes, of course," Hailey heard herself saying. "I'm sure it's very interesting. Uh—was Pete leaving at once?"

"Not right away," Hjalmar said. "He aimed to have himself a good time at Hackey's before he did anything else. That's where he was headed the last I saw him."

Not long ago, Hailey remembered, she had convinced herself that she was strong enough not only to endure but to rise above all torment. Suddenly, she knew that the future could be endurable only if there was hope that Pete would return.

Now all hope was gone.

10

THE TRAVELER'S RETURN

THE EARLY MORNING westbound Limited came to Spruce Crossing on exact schedule, and a brisk spurt of autumn wind whirled a miniature storm of leaves across the station platform. Pete Gant stepped from a slowly moving car squarely into the center of this. It was a good wind, he felt—in fact, everything was very good.

Pete set his face to this good north wind and gulped with hungry lungs. The wind had a tang, almost a taste, that set it apart from all others and marked it as clearly as needles mark a spruce. But suddenly it occurred to Pete that his usual summer malady had not descended even once. He'd never felt he could not breathe—but the summer just ended was remarkable for better reasons than that.

From day of arrival to day of departure, Pete had not set foot outside the city, and at one time "city" was a synonym for prison to him. But rather than the torture he'd always considered inevitable if he was ever hemmed in, he looked back on the happiest summer of his life. He could not explain why, but he knew that anything he'd found between book covers had contributed so little to remaking him and done so little to change him that it was better written off.

The answer lay elsewhere, but books were in no way at fault. The summer had been most rewarding and had taught him much. Among other things, it had forcefully driven home the fact that he was not a born scholar. However, he had also acquired enough appreciation of literature to concede the true value of the printed word.

Lots of people could see the sense and find the meaning in one book where others could not. Pete's favorite was *The Rubayait.* On the other hand, he had sweated ten stubborn days over *Paradise Lost* before conceding a hopeless battle. But it took a Casimir, a Hailey, or a George MacClain to explore the broad fields of all literature and still understand.

Books were a challenge, and maybe that's what had made the summer so very happy and so very short for Pete. Or it might have been the work. He had understated neither his ambitions nor conditions the first night he met George MacClain. Accustomed to starting his activities at sunrise and continuing to sundown, he saw no reason to change either his schedule or his hours simply because he was tackling books instead of trap lines. He'd found it necessary to set a pace his teacher could match. There were other adjustments.

Whatever it was and however he'd found it, Pete had acquired something he'd lacked and basically needed.

Down track, an impatient attendant leaned from the baggage car. Pop Hennessey, local baggage agent and almost as old as the truck he pulled, dawdled toward it. Pete fell in beside him.

"Give you a hand, Pop?"

"Hah!" The old man turned to glare. "I been haulin' this buggy a passel of years! Guess I can manage a mite longer!"

Pete said agreeably, "Sure, Pop."

"Step on it!" the fretful attendant urged.

Pop muttered under his breath and cut his speed in half. "Young whippersnapper!" he growled. "Thinks he's smart just 'cause he wears clean pants an' got a lazy man's job! In my day there'd been no room for the likes of him and no baggage for him to handle! We bought our goods to home or done without, like sensible folks. But when frills can be bought, people buy frills! World's all shot to bits these days!"

"Sure," Pete said amiably.

Pop came alongside the car, withered the attendant with a snarl and a scornful look, and staggered beneath the weight of a carton that was all but thrown into his arms.

"Let me," Pete said.

While Pop leaned against the truck, pushed his cap up on his forehead, and for once even forgot to growl, Pete piled the carton and nine more like it on the old truck. The baggage attendant thumbed through his papers.

"Now if we can get somebody to sign for these. Do you know a Pete Gant?"

"I'm Gant."

While Pete signed the receipt, Pop looked incredulously from him to the little mountain of cartons.

"What in thunder's that heavy!" he finally ejaculated. "You find a gold mine, too?"

"Could be," Pete said.

Pop muttered, "Well, they do say them as has gits. I might of knowed your luck was just started when you struck it rich in fur!"

Holding up a long and slender parcel, obviously containing a new rifle, the attendant interrupted. "Do you know a Hjalmar Toenesson?"

"Yep," answered Pete. "I'll sign for him, too."

"Thanks, mister." The attendant looked sourly at Pop. "If I had to run all this through Methuselah here we'd meet ourselves coming back."

Before Pop could frame a sufficiently scathing reply, the attendant rolled the door shut and the train went on its way. Pete laid Hjalmar's parcel beside his own. Having felt the weight of Pete's cartons, Pop stepped aside, somewhat less concerned over his vested rights in the baggage truck. Pete grinned, caught up the tongue, and pulled the loaded truck to Pop's baggage room.

"Well?" the old man demanded.

"Well what?"

"You aim to leave them boxes clutterin' up my wagon? Next train's due in two hours."

Pete promised, "They'll be moved before then."

"Better be," Pop muttered darkly, "or you'll find yourself in trouble aplenty. Interferin' with a railroad, that's what they'll call it. I–"

"Pete!" Hjalmar Toenesson's roar blasted Pop's voice into silence as its owner came around a corner of the station. He flung himself forward to pump Pete's extended hand and roared again. "I thought you'd be in Africa, or Texas, or some other foreign country!"

"I tried to run away but my feet wouldn't obey orders," Pete said. "They just naturally brought me right back here."

"Good!" Hjalmar beamed. His eyes lighted on the parcel. "Ha! My new rifle! You sign for it, Pete?"

"Yep."

"Thanks," Hjalmar said. "I wanted to meet the train but didn't quite make it. You goin' back trappin' this season?"

"I haven't even given it a thought," Pete said.

"You'll go," Hjalmar decided for him. "You can have your line back, too. Me an' Ole, we wouldn't even of thought to buy you out if we knew you'd come back. Anyhow, you can't be bought out until you're paid, an' you ain't been. Me an' Ole, we'll move back to our old line."

Pete asked, "Have you moved into mine?"

"Yah, but," Hjalmar shrugged, "we move out again. It's just a baby job."

"Oh, sure," Pete said caustically. "Even a one-armed baby could do it! If you and Ole work twenty hours a day, and wear out such horses as you don't kill, and are lucky enough to beat out deep snow, and get all the other breaks, you'll have everything in working order by December first, or thereabouts."

Hjalmar nodded. "Yah, we will."

"So," Pete continued, "I have an idea that beats yours forty-nine ways. Don't move at all."

Hjalmar asked bewilderedly, "You mean trap from Two Moose?"

"I mean trap from Two Moose."

"But–it's your line."

"It's *your* line," Pete corrected him. "I remember selling it to you and Ole."

Hjalmar asked dubiously, "You mean that?"

"Sure I mean it," Pete scoffed. "Do you think I'm like you flighty Swedes and change my mind every ten or so years?"

Hjalmar grinned appreciatively, and relief drove anxiety

from his eyes. To move now, with trapping about to start, almost guaranteed a lean season.

He murmured, "Well, if you're real sure."

"Are you all set at Two Moose?" Pete questioned.

"Yah. Me an' Ole, we worked in there an awful lot this summer."

"What's to be done?"

Hjalmar shrugged. "Move in."

"Can you make another pack trip?"

"Maybe a short one"—Hjalmar looked puzzled—"but there ain't any dudes."

"For me," Pete explained, "and I need a favor."

"For you," Hjalmar beamed, "me an' Ole will take time."

"The favor first," Pete said. "Can you loan me a rifle and sleeping bag, which you'll pick up later, and scrounge a grubstake that'll see me through to the Wisbayah?"

"Easy."

"Then," Pete indicated the cartons, "will you pack these out to the Zluskis'? They're as trail proof as they can be made. I packed them myself. But they're destructible and they must get there."

Hjalmar answered simply, "They will. What you goin' to do, Pete?"

"Get my outfit and go down the trail!" Pete told him happily.

Hjalmar frowned. "If you're in such a hurry, I can loan you a saddle horse, too."

"No, thanks," Pete declined the offer. "Horses are too slow. Oh! Will you stop at Tunk Abbot's and bring my dogs, too?"

"You ain't even taking them?" Hjalmar questioned.

"Nope," Pete declared. "I'm in a big hurry."

Hjalmar said dryly, "Don't look at me. I didn't say you ain't."

A half-hour later, having escaped Hjalmar's nine children by dint of an outright bribe that sent them whooping to the candy counter, and having reassured Hjalmar's wife that she was still the world's finest cook but he couldn't possibly wait until dinner was ready, Pete hit the trail.

11

MADNESS IN MAGIC LAND

AWAKING at her usual hour, Hailey Zluski turned toward her curtained window and was at once captivated by the sound of the wind. It was not sighing, she decided, or moaning, or screaming, or conforming to any traditional noises of conventional wind. The brisk September wind was snarling impudent threats of the havoc it proposed to work when winter came. Hailey shook her small fist defiantly at it—and grinned at herself for doing so, but the gesture was wholly in keeping with her frame of mind. She would defy the wind and all other challenges, and never once feel inadequate. If nothing else, the summer had taught her the infinite strength of a human spirit.

The weakly-lighted window brightened as the new day stretched its sinews and found its strength. Hailey's memory took her back to the first visit of the Toenesson brothers, and the fateful news that had crushed her final hope about Pete. She had not slept at all that night, but lay in numb despair to watch the last light fade from her window shortly before midnight and the first light return shortly after that. She had been very sure that each day to come would be an eternity within itself, and seem never to end. But they had ended, and, on the whole, they had passed swiftly enough. Once again, the impossible had proved quite possible. The intolerable, even though one could not always submit with an humble heart and meek spirit, could be tolerated and somehow the window with its light symbolized this, even while it became a sure and infallible guide.

That light was a fundamental truth, a basic foundation too firm to be shaken and too powerful to be changed. It had begun when time began and would endure until time ended. For all his ingenuity, it was a miracle no man could hope to match and it was more precise than the finest watch that the most skilled artisan could devise. It was beauty, inspiration, and assurance of immortality. The morning light on the window was not concerned with weeks, months, seasons, or years. It belonged to the days only.

One who knew and loved it could not truly think of monotonous days, for there were none. The light that came at different times each day made each day different, so there couldn't possibly be monotonous years. Although one could not avoid mortal ills, only the dull would ever find life futile, or even boring.

In spite of the fact that she could not pinpoint any one day, or even a general succession of days, Hailey felt that she had recently slipped out of one intriguing land to go live in another of equal fascination. If there was a single reason to regret such a move, it was the pain of its utter finality. There was not even a very faint possibility of going back. As compensation, those who lived in this advanced world were granted suitable strength and confidence to live well in it. If they could not heal some wounds, or even find any salve that would lessen the pain, their strength was equal to bearing them.

Presently, Hailey heard her father come into the kitchen and build the morning fire. She lay quietly until it was built, for this was one of her few remaining expedients that never failed. She had needed all the ingenuity at her command to shift burdens from Casimir's shoulders to her own, and, at the same time, convince her father that he still carried his full load. It was not always easy. Although there was much she could do, some tasks were simply out of the question. For example, she had worried endlessly about their winter's supply of wood.

Casimir should not cut it and she could not. Finally, on one of their various stopovers while going to or from Pete's trap line, she head Hjalmar Toenesson say he needed another rifle and offered him hers in exchange for some wood.

The offer was neither accepted nor rejected, but their next time through the brothers stopped, set up a buzz saw and gasoline engine whose disassembled parts were distributed among various pack horses, fueled their engine from drums carried by other horses, and dragged in and sawed up enough wood for three winters. Then, grinning, they each stole a bashful kiss from each of Hailey's cheeks, declared they were paid in full, took everything apart, put it back on the horses, and proceeded to their own camp.

That solved one major problem. Another, even more formidable, must be solved, however. Hailey had been as thrifty as she knew how, which included gracing the Zluski board with trout so often that Casimir said he was growing fins. But if trout as a staple were not as exciting as a gourmet's occasional delight, they were free for the catching.

In spite of all Hailey could do, though, there remained certain necessities that only money could buy, and the fact that she intended to confine her shopping list to bare essentials did not suggest where she might get any money to pay for them. But although it must be faced, preferably in time to let the Toenessons bring what was needed before snow closed the trail to all except dog traffic, it could be put off for a while, at least. Pete Gant had brought an unusual store of staples and Hailey saw no good reason why she shouldn't use them.

She rose, dressed—and suddenly felt rebellious. It was a feeling she must conquer, she reminded herself as she started toward the kitchen. Rebellion was a luxury she could not afford. But, instead of conquering it as usual, she was hopelessly conquered and providing herself with a number of logical arguments as to why she should yield to the impulse, before she even reached the kitchen door.

It was not as though she intended to ignore her obligations, she reassured herself. All she wanted was one holiday, and she wouldn't even think of that much if it meant neglecting anything at all. But everything was in order. Folly could take care of the sheep for one day and the horses always took care of themselves. She would see that her father had an adequate breakfast and be back in time to cook his supper. He wouldn't mind getting his own lunch.

Doubly exciting because of this hair-trigger spontaneity, the notion captured her delighted fancy. She hadn't gone gypsying since last fall, when she had rambled in her own private world and accidentally found the great bull moose. How could she be sure that this world no longer existed, as she had come to believe lately, when she hadn't even been to find out for herself? Wrapped in a wonderful dream, she found herself in the kitchen with no clear idea as to just how she'd come there and heard her father's greeting.

"Hela!"

Startled, and feeling a bit foolish, she turned to face him. "Uh– Yes, Dad?"

Casimir's gentle smile seemed to cast a soft glow over his rugged features. Hailey felt herself blushing. Her father laughed.

"What were you thinking of?" he queried.

"Why– Why–" Confusion left her speechless.

"So do not even try to tell it," her father advised. "Your face could not have looked as it did unless your heart bade it. And the heart's wishes come true only if they're secret."

Hailey giggled. "I must have been sleepwalking!"

"So," Casimir said serenely. "Then I think it well to sleep-walk more, if it makes you so happy. Should you awaken, and look for me, I will be in my study all day. There is some research I must do."

Hailey's heart leaped. Some kindly angel had surely smiled upon her. First, the sudden mighty yearning for a holiday, then the one obstacle that might have kept her home was an obstacle no longer. Her father never needed her when he worked in his study.

Suddenly she was stricken by another thought and glanced at him. He was very good and very wise. Was he wise enough to read her very thoughts, and from them to know her secret wish? Was his plan to spend the day in his study as sudden as her great desire for a holiday, and his professed research a pretext to set her free? Hailey saw nothing in his expression to indicate this.

Breakfast over, Casimir went immediately to his study. Hailey washed the dishes, packed a lunch, caught up her rifle, and fared forth to determine, once and for all, if her world of magic still existed. She'd go down the river, she decided, toward the range of the great bull. If she was lucky, she might even see him again.

The spruces closed behind her, and the instant they did she knew that her magic was indeed no more. They had ceased to be a sheltering screen that surrounded her private world, wherein she was sole mistress and to make a wish was to see it granted. Even though she suspected from the first moment that fighting her loss was futile and that, eventually, she must yield to it, Hailey struggled against the feeling. The change came from herself, she argued firmly. A child had come this way before, and the world of magic was so much easier to see because the eyes of a child never have trouble seeing such things. A woman walked here now, and, although an adult's eyes were not so keen, she would still see the magic if she looked hard enough.

A nagging voice that refused to be silent crumbled her every argument with an unassailable fact. If there was any basis for what she was trying to make herself believe, she might have anything she wanted. How was that possible, when she could never have what she wanted most? Did she really think she could deceive herself? Wasn't it silly to try?

She strove with near desperation to make her mind reject what so obviously was and recapture what had been. It seemed a losing battle, but she dared not yield. She *must* find again what she had found here so many times, for if she failed, she

would never have the courage to try again. Nor would a compromise suffice; she must conquer completely or her heart would die.

Hailey walked slowly, determined to miss nothing. She stopped, wondering if she should eat her lunch near the same log upon which she had been sitting when she saw first the snowshoe hare and then the great bull. Somehow, she seemed to be facing a terrible decision, as though the smallest act had a suddenly vast potential for good or evil, and only by completing the act would she know which result she had brought upon herself. If she chose wrongly, she must accept the consequences. If rightly, she would reap the benefits.

The matter was of such grave concern that she stood for a

very long while, wavering as to whether she should sit down on the log, return to the house, or continue her walk. Presently, she set her jaw and fought to be free of the daze that enfolded her like a clinging net, so tightly wrapped that even her mind was no longer hers. She was both ashamed and angry to admit that she had deliberated so profoundly over anything so inconsequential. As though it mattered whether she sat down, turned back, or went on! Again mistress of herself, Hailey prepared to step over the log and seat herself. Abruptly, she froze in her tracks.

When she saw him again he was no more than a yard or so from where she'd seen him the first time, but, although he was in the same place, surely it was not the same bull! That one had been a placid creature, a dull brute with scarcely more fire than an ordinary barnyard bull. He had been notable only for his sheer size and brute mass, as a lofty mountain is notable but the foothills about it are not. Aside from that, with his unbalanced, grotesque, single-antlered head and his lusty indulgence of appetite, he had been more ludicrous than fierce. If he had known she was near, he would have fled as readily as any timid rabbit. He was then the epitome of an image that sprang to mind when she thought of most wild things, all animal.

This bull was no more like that one than a January blizzard

is like a June rain. He was all devil. At the very peak of his strength and power, ablaze with the lust of the rut, he was ferocity incarnate. His great antlers were perfectly balanced, and when the bull turned his head they moved with the rhythmic precision of a boxer's hand. A sleek hide was tight over a frame that was not the shapeless mass she remembered, but streamlined as a torpedo.

Hailey trembled, and did not attempt to deny that a terrible fear made her shiver. Of the many bull moose she'd seen, no more than a half dozen had stood their ground longer than a few seconds, and those were in the madness of the rut when she had come upon them. But even rutting bulls ran as soon as their hot senses cooled enough to tell them a human was near. Once she had chanced upon two fighting bulls that broke and scurried away the second they realized she was watching them.

She tried to moisten her dry lips with a dry tongue, the while she was almost staggered by the realization that, at last, she knew why she could no longer find her world of magic. It had been destroyed by a fiend in the guise of this bull. No wonder Pete Gant hated and was determined to destroy such a thing!

Hailey fought her way back to the world of reality. She was looking at a bull moose, she told herself, nothing more or less. He seemed to be different from other bulls partly because of his size and partly because, as she saw, he was the very symbol of brute savagery and power. It was as though some sculptor with genius at his fingertips had created a statue of the great bull in such a manner that it expressed the brute, then some malicious god had breathed life into the statue.

A moment later, Hailey saw the cow. Almost black where

the bull was near tan, a bit ragged where he was seal sleek, and meek as he was arrogant, she stepped from behind a tree and walked on the far side of the bull, so that her foreparts were hidden and only her hindquarters jutted out behind him. He turned imperiously toward the cow.

Recovering her composure, Hailey chided herself for being afraid with no good reason. Before her stood only another manifestation of the ancient miracle, that, at the same time, is all hope and all history. There was something about it as solidly comforting as the light on her bedroom window.

Suddenly, the bull swung to face her and grunted. Hailey felt a little chagrin. She must have been careless enough to betray herself. Then, bristling, grunting, fuming, the monster launched his attack. As she raised her rifle, her first and strongest impression was that she now saw the bull as Pete Gant must have seen it. Then she started shooting, holding steadily and aiming carefully to make every bullet count.

After the third shot, with the bull neither slowing nor even flinching, she knew clearly that the two cartridges remaining in her rifle would never bring him down in time.

12

BROUGHT HOME

DAYBREAK was no more than a faint gray promise in the black sky when Pete Gant awoke. He crawled out of his sleeping bag, laced his pacs, and stood with his back to the wind as he spooned cold beans into his mouth and gulped cold bacon and biscuits. It had proved worthwhile, when he stopped to cook his supper, to cook enough for breakfast, too. He needn't delay to build a morning fire and he'd only miss tea. Pete grinned briefly. He'd always thought a trail man's tea second in importance to his breathing, but it was third.

Pete shouldered his pack, caught up his rifle, and turned his face to the biting north wind as he swung up the trail. Hjalmar Toenesson had suspected first his sincerity and then his mentality when the young trapper declared he could make better time without horses or dogs to slow him down. But Hjalmar was not one to deviate from the traditional and Pete knew what he was talking about.

Despite an undoubted superiority for short spurts, Pete had yet to see a horse that could equal a man when it came to a gruelling, purposeful journey. Dogs would have provided nothing except company on this snowless trail. Either horses or dogs would have considered themselves entitled to rest at the day's end, and thereafter they would not have traveled at all unless they were coaxed or coerced.

Leaving Spruce Crossing shortly after eight o'clock the previous morning, Pete reached halfway Cabin, thirty miles out, an hour before dark. After stopping to cook and for a brief rest, he had decided to push on for another ten miles–and had continued for twenty before weariness forced him to camp and sleep. Now he was within ten miles of the Zluskis' and should reach them in time for a late breakfast. No animal would have been satisfied to maintain such a pace and some would not have been equal to it. Man was the superior of beasts in more ways than one.

Somewhat curiously, it occurred to Pete that he had made this same journey one year ago to the exact day. Recalling that other trip brought recollections of the great bull that had treed him and that he had almost forgotten. Once he'd burned to kill him, and he'd still do so if he could, but he would kill for food or the magnificent trophy. Of course, there would be some personal satisfaction, but killing the moose merely because he had chased him up a tree and kept him there all night was no longer of primary importance.

He had not understood–and still didn't understand–Hailey's defense of the bull or any reason for her ultimatum that night he had found her waiting at the scow landing and unexpectedly kissed her. But he no longer kept on wondering about it. Among other things, the summer had taught him that there was much he did not understand. That was no reason for shame–if it were properly accepted and viewed in a proper perspective. No man, not even George MacClain, knew everything.

Pete had clarified another matter to such an extent that he would never again question or hesitate in whatever concerned it. That night Hailey had asked him if he could think of nothing except revenge on the great bull, and he had told her he'd been yearning to do something else. Then he had obliged with a demonstration and kissed her. Well, he hadn't been yearning. He hadn't even thought of kissing her then—at least in any definitive terms, but he'd given the subject considerable thought since. If nothing else, the next kiss he gave her would be shadowed by no false pretense—always supposing, of course, that there would be a next time.

Hailey had been frigidly aloof ever since that night at the landing and there was no reason to suppose she'd be otherwise now. There weren't even reasonable grounds to think she cared if he ever came back . . . but he could not stay away. He'd discovered that no man can be a free man if he leaves his heart behind him. He had fully intended to go away—where made little difference—maybe to Alaska, Australia, wherever he could find country that he liked.

Far places still had a certain tantalizing allure, but now he knew that, no matter where he went or what he did, unless his heart went with him and was of him, he could hope for nothing more solid than the vapors that rose fromh chill waters in the dawn. He'd gone to George MacClain in the hope that he might learn whatever it was he must know when he finally went back to Hailey. All he'd truly learned was that he must go back—but that was enough for him.

Coming to the pool where he'd stumbled and left his mud-choked rifle just before the great bull charged, Pete crossed without interrupting his stride. Even if there was another rutting bull with an inclination to charge, there were no dogs to push him this time and the rifle in his hands was Hjalmar's own cherished 30-06. Armed with that, he'd face any moose—or anything else that cared to dispute the path.

The sun was bright when Pete came to the Zluski clearing, but the cold north wind still whispered of frigid weather soon to come and the day lacked summer gentleness. He halted to study the scene before him.

Although he had left in late spring and was returning in early autumn, he had a strangely disquieting impression that he had departed only yesterday. Stationed a discreet distance from the forest and any sudden surprise that might emerge from the forest, Folly watched over his flock. The horses were foraging near the river. Stacks of hay—and who had stacked them—were in the usual places. With the scow at its landing and the house unchanged, a summer couldn't possibly have come and gone. There should be something different.

Suddenly, Pete staggered before a crushing wave of doubt. The whole journey somehow seemed silly and futile. Surely the Zluskis must know that he'd sold his trap line, which alone would tell them that he had no intention of coming back. What, besides restrained amusement, would they feel when he returned for the sole purpose of courting Hailey? How would he even begin to explain his summer with George MacClain, or why he had chosen such a summer? If, as seemed most probable, they took him seriously, what about the lack of letters from him? Should he expect them to believe that he'd started and torn up at least twenty because the words he put on paper never said what he wanted to say?

Resolutely, Pete went on. There was no assurance whatever that he would win—or even be made welcome. But it was better to find out what might be than to turn back and forever after wonder what might have been.

As soon as Pete came into the clearing, Folly roared his challenge and, a moment later, rifle in hand, Casimir Zluski appeared at the door. He immediately ducked back into the house. Nothing threatened, so he wanted to put his rifle away. A nagging anxiety and a cold fear stirred Pete's heart. Hailey had not come to the door with her father. Why not? If Hailey Zluski never married, it would not be for lack of suitors—and anything might have happened during the long summer. Pete berated himself for ever leaving Hailey, and conjured up a dozen different mental images of the man who was now her husband. Or was she married? She was still so very young. . . . But girls were apt to marry very early in this wilderness country.

Pete quickened his pace because he must know very soon. Casimir came outside and greeted him with a hearty, "Welcome, Pete."

Pete stopped again, suddenly helpless to say anything that even hinted of common sense. Wordlessly, he searched Casimir's face for the news he must have. He saw nothing he could translate, but he never had been able to read Casimir's face. He was sure only that the summer had indeed brought change—at least to Hailey's father. An extended absence revealed sharply what day-to-day familiarity tended to hide. Casimir was noticeably more gaunt and drawn than he had been.

Finally, Pete found his voice. "I came back, Casimir."

It seemed a wholly inadequate statement, the lamest of ways to express the urge that had spurred him on the trail. It was as though he had tried to kill a moose with a slingshot. Also, the remark was entirely superfluous. Besides seeing for himself that Pete was back, somehow Casimir seemed always to have known that he would come. Now he should remark about it, but he said only, "I'm glad you're here, Pete."

Casimir spoke in riddles that compounded Pete's bewilderment—but he did not speak lightly or with even a trace of condescending tolerance.

Pete said recklessly, "There is something you should know, Casimir. Last fall, before freeze-up, I came down the river just about dark and found Hailey at the landing. I—I kissed her!"

He braced for the explosion that must follow. When Casimir did nothing except continue to look at him with calm eyes, Pete wondered if the other had heard.

He asked, "Did you hear me?"

"I heard," Casimir answered quietly, "but I'll not do as you expect. Your great mistake was in failing to kiss her again."

"What!" Pete gasped.

"You are in love with her, aren't you?"

"Yes!"

Facing Casimir squarely, Pete shouted the admission as though it must be challenged. Somehow, he hoped it would be. He would know how to fight an angered or enraged Casimir. He could do nothing at all about this cool-eyed man whose strength lay in his power to think.

"Then why did you leave?" Casimir asked.

Pete answered seriously, "Because I had to. Hailey hated me from the night I kissed her, although not nearly so much as I hated myself for betraying your hospitality in such a manner."

"So?" Pete thought he saw a glint of amusement in Casimir's eyes. "May I ask a personal question?"

"Go ahead."

"How did Hela react to your kiss?"

Pete said, "I don't understand."

"Was she offended—or annoyed?"

Pete said bluntly, "I've never figured what she was. All she said was that if ever I shot the bull moose that ran me up a tree, no matter what the reason, I must never come near her again."

Casimir queried, "What did you say to that?"

"I got on my high horse—and I sure wish I hadn't," Pete answered ruefully. "I told her I'd make a special point of killing that bull and make her a present of the head."

"Were you serious?"

"I thought I was," Pete admitted, "but I could have killed the bull very shortly after that and didn't."

"Why didn't you tell Hela?"

"I didn't see how it could make a difference. I was a fool."

Casimir said gently, "That's scarcely a mark of distinction. Most young people are fools. In selling your trap line, and in letting Hjalmar Toenesson think you intended to go to some far country, you went on and burned all the rest of your bridges. Hela never expects to see you again."

The reply, so different from what he had expected, left Pete bewildered. He blurted out, "Surely you knew I'd come?"

"I hoped you would come," Casimir corrected him. "I could not know, for I could know nothing of the way God made your heart."

Pete said, "I wanted to go away, the farther the better. Then I found that, no matter how many miles lay between us, I'd still be here with Hailey. Can you understand that?"

"I can," Casimir assured him. "When did you discover it for yourself?"

"The same day I talked with Hjalmar," Pete said. "I went to Hackey's and tried to have some fun—but it didn't work out that way. That's when I first knew I must come back here."

"Yet you delayed," Casimir pointed out.

"I wanted to be able to offer something when I came," Pete explained. "I thought that, if in addition to asking Hailey to share my world, it would mean more if I tried to share hers. I went east to Royalton and found a teacher, Professor George MacClain, and asked him to teach me what you and Hailey find in books."

"Did he?" Casimir asked.

"No," Pete admitted, "but that isn't his fault, because he certainly tried. I'm not even sure I can learn any more, but I'm willing to try, if Hailey cares to teach me. I bought books that Professor MacClain recommended. The Toenessons are packing them out here."

"So that was your summer fling?" Casimir inquired.

Pete said, "That's all of it, and I'll not beat around the bush with you. I intend to marry Hailey if she'll have me."

"A splendid idea," Casimir murmured.

"You mean you won't object?"

"Quite the contrary, Pete. I'll approve most heartily, I'd choose you as my son-in-law if I could. Unfortunately, however, mine is not the choice that counts.

"Then I may see Hailey?"

"You may indeed," Casimir assured him. "You must wait, though. Hela went for a stroll in the woods this morning and she never returns before evening."

Pete asked eagerly, "Which way did she go?"

"Down river."

"I'll find her!"

Pete turned and ran across the clearing. Casimir watched him go, and if his eyes were a little sad for the follies of youth, they were light and gay for the crushing burden he need carry no longer. As a man, it had been easy for him to recognize a young man in love, but all his erudition and great experience had taught him nothing of women. True, he had known when Hailey entered the kitchen this morning that she yearned for a change. There was no need to ask what change. A lonely holiday in the forest was the only one available. Without her knowledge, her father had noted the direction she took.

Casimir's smile still lingered and his heart beat high. He had not known about the kiss, but now he need know nothing more to decide what he had hitherto merely suspected. Hailey

returned Pete's love and it was good. Now let them find each other in the loneliness of the forest—and then never again be lonely.

Pacs flying, the rifle in his hand seeming weightless, Pete ran through the forest because he could not walk. He seemed

somehow to have become conqueror of all obstacles and master of whatever offered to interfere.

Anything but an unbroken sweep, the forest had as many divisions and separations as a city. There were thickets, windfalls, swamps, ledges, streams. Even wild animals would not try to enter the more forbidding places. He knew that Hailey would stay on the moose trails that kept her near the river. The ease of getting lost and the dangers involved were an old story to her, but she couldn't possibly go astray if she could always find the river.

Pete also realized that a stroll around the block was not for Hailey when alluring miles beckoned. She might go a very long way before turning back.

The sun was approaching high noon when Pete heard her first shot. He did not pause to listen and there was no need to interpret. With plenty of game around the home clearing, Hailey would never come this far to hunt and she would never shoot wantonly. That shot had a voice of its own that screamed of deadly peril for the girl.

Pete doubled his speed. He heard the second shot, then the third and fourth, and breathed a prayer. Hailey's rifle held only five shots. Furthermore, only with the wildest luck would five shots, or twice five, from such a light rifle stop a charging grizzly or moose. . . .

Pete flung himself around a copse of trees and saw Hailey, standing steady behind her log, holding the final shot for the nearest possible range. The great bull, not visibly injured, was less than twenty yards from her and coming fast. Pete raised Hjalmar's big rifle and tried not to think that he would have no second chance. He took almost casual aim, squeezed the trigger, and heard the blast.

For the following second he dared not look. Finally forcing his eyes to tell him what must be and was already beyond change, he saw Hailey still standing. No more than twice the length of her rifle in front of her, the great bull lay on the ground. An upthrust leg moved feebly.

Pete walked forward so quietly that she did not hear him until he said, "Hello, Hailey."

She whirled. "Pete!"

Pete looked again at the dead bull and saw only an inert mass. There had been no joy in killing him, but only thankfulness because he had been killed in time. Hatred never should have entered into this. One did not hate an unreasoning brute.

Pete said, "I knew he was here and I could have killed him last winter–but I didn't. Now I wish I had."

"No, Pete," Hailey said.

The cow, that had run off with the first shot, but was waiting in the spruces for the bull to join her, grunted. She grunted a second time and thereafter was silent. The bull was dead–and yet he would live again. His flesh alone was mortal.

Hailey and Pete stepped nearer each other. Then all the magic was back again. The portals of Hailey's private world, that never had been wiped out at all but must now be seen by two pairs of eyes or not at all, opened for them. The kiss that followed was joyfully given and taken. Both of them had been thinking about it for a very long time.

JIM KJELGAARD

was born in New York City. Happily enough, he was still in the pre-school age when his father decided to move the family to the Pennsylvania mountains. There young Jim grew up among some of the best hunting and fishing in the United States. He commented: "If I had pursued my scholastic duties as diligently as I did deer, trout, grouse, squirrel, etc., I might have had better report cards!"

Jim Kjelgaard worked at various jobs—trapper, teamster, guide, surveyor, factory worker and laborer. When he was in his late twenties, he decided to become a full-time writer. He succeeded in his wish. Several hundred of his short stories and articles and quite a few books for young people have been published.

He indicated his favorite hobbies as hunting, fishing, life-long interest in conservation, dogs and questing for new stories. He has described some of these searches in this way: "Story hunts have led me from the Atlantic to the Pacific and from the Arctic Circle to Mexico City. Stories, like gold, are where you find them. You may discover one three thousand miles from home or, as in *The Spell of the White Sturgeon* and *Hi Jolly!*, right on your own door step."